BROKEN CREEK

Walt Gallatin, young owner of the Spur S ranch, walked into an ambush at the Broken Latigo Saloon. Lucky for him, Tobacco Jones was there to save his neck — but both men knew there'd be a next time. Big Val Marcus wanted the Spur S and, with a brace of hired guntoughs, would do anything to get it. The showdown with Marcus threatened to explode into a full-scale range war, unless Gallatin and Tobacco Jones could stop the trouble at the source!

Walt Gallatin, young owner of the Spur S ranch, walked into an ambush at the Broken Range Saloon. Lucky for him, Tobacco Jones was there to save his neck — but how much longer could be a next time? Big Val Marcus wanted the Spur S and, with a brace of hired gunslingers, would do anything to get it. The showdown with Marcus threatened to explode into a full-scale range war unless Gallatin and Tobacco Jones could stop the trouble at the source!

LINFORD
Leicester

LEE FLOREN

◆

BROKEN CREEK

Complete and Unabridged

LINFORD
Leicester

First published in the
United States of America

First Linford Edition
published March 1995

British Library CIP Data

Floren, Lee
    Broken Creek.—Large print ed.—
Linford western library
I. Title II. Series
813.52 [F]

ISBN 0-7089-7692-1

Published by
F. A. Thorpe (Publishing) Ltd.
Anstey, Leicestershire

Set by Words & Graphics Ltd.
Anstey, Leicestershire
Printed and bound in Great Britain by
T. J. Press (Padstow) Ltd., Padstow, Cornwall

This book is printed on acid-free paper

THEY had their trap set in the Broken Latigo Saloon, and the man they intended to kill was young Walt Gallatin, the Broken Creek rancher. Just now Walt Gallatin was upstairs over the saloon talking to his lawyer, John Wimberley. And down below the trap was set; the gunmen were in their places.

Val Marcus, big and scowling, stood with his broad back against the bar, elbows hooked over the railing, his grey-green eyes on the stairway down which Walt Gallatin would come. His big Stetson was pushed back to show his dark thick hair, and his muscular body, hard and solid, was in the prime of life — for Val Marcus was thirty-six. He owned the big Rocking R Ranch and ran his whitefaces the length and width of Singletree Basin. He had bought the outfit two years before and shipped in his own crew of riders.

They were tough cowboys.

Down the bar about ten feet, also watching the stairway, stood Lew Basick. Lew Basick was Val Marcus' range boss. A tall man in his early forties, his leathery face showed the effects of the cow trail, and crow's feet heemed in his pale eyes. His eyebrows were white — the silken white of an albino — and his trim moustache was silken white, too. He also had his cream-colored Stetson pushed back, and the late afternoon sun, slanting through the high glass window, showed sparse hair the color of pulled toffee. He wore a red shirt, pleated and gaudy, and his *Californio* pants were neatly pressed. His gun-harness was black and smooth and polished, the brass rims of the cartridges glistening — his boots were highly polished, too.

Lew Basick was a range dandy. Lew Basick was also a killer.

Val Marcus sent his glance to the

man who sat at the poker table, to the right of the stairs. He was a Rocking R rider known only as Blacky. Now his heavy brows were pulled down into a scowl, for he faced the sun too much. He moved to the left and got the sun out of his eyes.

"Look good at that sun, Blacky," Marcus said quietly. "Some day you won't see it. That day, friend, could be today . . ."

"Close your mouth," Blacky said.

Lew Basick spoke. "The man's touchy, Boss." His silken white moustache moved with his slow smile.

"Nothing from you either, Lew," Blacky said irritably.

Marcus shrugged and killed the conversation. Across the rutted street, thick with dust, a man loafed on the bench in front of the Mercantile, dark in the growing shade. Marcus looked at Jim Crow and marked his position and found it good. If Walt Gallatin, by some miracle, got past him, and past Lew Basick and Blacky — well, he'd run into Jim Crow.

And Jim Crow could take care of himself.

Marcus let his eyes rest on a buckskin horse tied to the pine-pole hitchrack. The buckskin, a tough trail-horse, weighed about thirteen hundred pounds. He was a line-back with a black mane and tail. Marcus could see the brand on his right shoulder — the Spur S. The Spur S was Walt Gallatin's iron.

The Rocking R owner, seemingly satisfied, pulled his glance back into the Broken Latigo Saloon. Behind the long bar, the bartender was pounding on the bung of a beer barrel, the rap of his bung-starter loud in the afternoon stillness.

"Enough of that noise, Smokey," Marcus growled.

"Go to blazes." Smokey kept on pounding. The barrel lay on a rack, bung upright.

Blacky glanced angrily at Marcus. "The fool is stubborn."

4

Marcus ordered, "Get out, Smokey!"

Smokey held the bung-starter belligerently. "Can you make me run out of my own saloon, cowman?"

Marcus' face pulled down in anger. He almost started around the bar, then checked himself. "Smokey, where are your eyes? In your levis?"

"What'd you mean?"

Lew Basick's moustache moved again. "He's stubborn," the range boss said, "and besides that, he's dumb."

Smokey said, "You want me to man-handle you, Basick?"

For a second Lew Basick's faded eyes showed something brass and metallic. Then Val Marcus shook his head slowly. Basick settled back, tough and hard.

"Let the fool stay," Basick said.

There was another man — a stranger — also in the Broken Latigo. He had been in the saloon when Marcus and Basick and Blacky had entered, trailing Walt Gallatin. He still sat at a distant table, playing solitaire.

Val Marcus judged this man to be close to fifty. He was thin and over six feet tall, and his face was long and marred by deep wrinkles that seemed almost to encircle his tired-looking eyes. A Sioux jacket, made of buckskin and trimmed with dyed porcupine quills, hung around his gaunt, pointed shoulders and covered a blue denim shirt that was stuck into old levis now gray due to many washings. His boots were old, heels run over, and his spurs were a dull gray, evidently the product of some cow outfit's blacksmith.

He looked like a seedy range bum, Marcus decided.

Marcus said, "Stranger, you'd better leave."

The lanky man kept on playing solitaire and didn't look up.

Marcus repeated, "Stranger, I'm talking to you. You'd better hightail out of here."

This time the stranger looked up from his cards. His eyes, Marcus saw, had once been blue, but time had dulled the color, making them a pale gray. "You talking to me, feller?"

"Yes, you." Val Marcus spoke deliberately. "Come any minute now a man is coming down those stairs yonderly — a man who's to account to me, savvy. You might stop a stray slug. You'd better hightail out."

The tall man riffled the cards off the table. He asked, "Is that an order, friend?"

Marcus shook his head. "A suggestion." He had the impression this lanky stranger didn't cotton to taking orders.

The tall man got to his feet. He looked at the bartender. "So it's a su'prise party, eh?" He did not wait for an answer. "You leavin', Smokey?"

"I own this bar."

The tall man said to Marcus, "Thanks, feller," and he walked out the back door. But once outside in the alley, he lost his slowness. He ran down the alley, and when he came around the corner of the feed-barn he ran into a heavy-set woman who carried a big suitcase.

The woman dropped the suitcase on her foot. She had a heavy face with black hair in coils on her head, her hat set on these coils. A high ostrich feather lifted from the hat and ran down to touch the middle of her broad back. She had on a black silk dress, and the lanky man got a whiff of perfume.

"You darn fool!" she stormed. "You almost broke my foot!"

"I never stepped on you."

She stood on one leg, trying to reach her injured foot. But she was stiffly laced and couldn't quite make it. "No, but you made me drop my suitcase!"

The lanky man picked up the suitcase. It was terribly heavy. He wondered how the bottom stayed in it. "What you got in there?"

"Lead, mostly."

He stared. "Lead? Bullets?"

"No, not bullets! What do you think I am, a gunman? There's lead type in there; that's why it's so heavy! Oh, my instep!"

The lanky man could wait no longer. He gasped out, "I'm right sorry, ma'am," and ran down the street, the heavy-set woman looking after him in wonder. The stage from Cheyenne had just got into Singletree town — evidently the heavy woman had arrived on it — and he skirted the people standing on the sidewalk, running for the courthouse, there at the end of the single main street.

The courthouse, the single imposing building in Singletree, was a two-story affair, made of adobe, a material seldom used for buildings in southern Wyoming Territory. From what the lanky man had heard, the building had been built by itinerant Mexican laborers, who knew the secret of mixing adobe brick. But he wasn't thinking of that now, for he was puffing from his run. And the sun, although low, still held heat.

He found the big double-door open and he ran into a dimly lighted corridor, his boots pounding on the concrete floor. He went around a corner and, for the second time, ran into another person. This time the smash-up was with a thin, lanky man, almost as tall as he, and his force doubled the man, making him grunt in pain.

"For blaze's sake, Jones, look where you're goin', huh?"

"Sorry, Sher'ff Bennett. Where's Bates?"

"Bates? You mean *Judge* Bates?"

"Where is he?"

"In the judges' corridor, I guess."

The lanky man fell to a walk, leaving the sheriff coughing behind him. A faint smile touched Tobacco Jones' lips. He came to a door marked HAMILTON WASHBURN, JUDGE, FIFTH TERRITORIAL DISTRICT, and he went inside, disdaining to knock. The blinds had been pulled low and the light was dim inside.

The chair was wide and strong, with a hardwood back and with a thick swivel spring. It had to be a stout chair

10

to hold its burden — a stocky man with wide shoulders and broad of beam. The hand-tooled boots were resting on the maple desk, their silver-inlaid spurs, with saw-tooth rowels, lying beside the boots. Tobacco Jones ran his glance up the well-creased trousers, crammed into the half-boots, and still upward to the well-tailored coat, open now to show the white silk shirt underneath. The man's flat-brimmed black Stetson hung from the jaw-straps, now down around the husky, tanned throat, and the eyes were closed in sleep.

The black bow tie moved up and down with the husky man's Adam's apple as he snored, his thick lips slack and his mouth a little open. Tobacco Jones shook him roughly by the shoulder.

"Judge Bates, there's hell a poppin' in the Broken Latigo Saloon! Listen, Bates, I tell you, there's goin' be trouble!"

Judge Lemanuel Bates stirred, eyes still closed.

"Bates, damn it, wake up!"

The eyes opened then. They took in the lanky Tobacco Jones, who was biting off a chew of Horseshoe.

"Get out of here and let me sleep, Tobacco."

Tobacco had torn off his chew. "Bates, they got young Walt Gallatin penned in, an' they aim to cut him down! They got him upstairs in the Broken Latigo and when he comes down, they'll kill him!"

"Who's the *they*?"

"Val Marcus, and his gun-hands!"

The highly-polished boots swung off the desk, their peg-heels hitting the concrete floor. The chair creaked as the heavy body became upright. Judge Bates reached under the desk and took out his whisky jug and uncorked it. He ran a flat hand across the mouth of the heavy jug and studied his partner.

"You mean that, Tobacco?"

Tobacco Jones spat at a cuspidor in the corner and missed and Judge

Lem Bates gave him a hard look. "Too dark in here for accuracy," the lanky man apologized. "Bates, we gotta get down to the Broken Latigo right now!"

2

FOR once Judge Lemanuel Bates, in his haste, forgot his jug. Taking three steps to Tobacco Jones' two, the partners hurried down the corridor. Sheriff Rube Bennett, still coughing, looked at them, marveling at their haste.

"Fire some place, men?" he asked respectfully.

The judge said crisply, "Yes, in some housewife's cookstove, sir," and Sheriff Bennett looked sharply at their retreating backs, wondering if the judge's brain had slipped its picket-pin. His deputy, who had been in the office, heard the conversation, and suddenly broke out laughing. Bennett scowled darkly and went into his office, no smile on his homely face.

They reached the main street, and Tobacco Jones said, talking around his

14

chew, "They're waitin' at the foot of the stairs, Judge, an' young Walt Gallatin is upstairs, talking with his lawyer. What do we do?"

"You go in the front," the jurist said. "I'll go in the back. Your shotgun is at the hotel lobby; grab it as you go by. Mine is back in the stable on my saddle, and I'll procure it as I hurry by."

Tobacco spat a brown stream. "Sounds like a logical plan," he said.

They parted company, the heavy-set jurist running into the alley. His bronc nickered as he entered the stable, but this time Judge Bates had no sugar for the sugar-crazy animal; he jerked his sawed-off shotgun from the boot of the saddle that hung by one stirrup from a wooden wall-peg. He hurried out into the afternoon light, breaking the breech of the double-tubed weapon; he saw the dull gleam of two unfired shotgun cartridges and he snapped the lock tight. And all this time, although he hurried, he waited for the roar of gunfire.

For he knew sure as he faced death and taxes, that Val Marcus and his killer-crew aimed to kill young Walt Gallatin. For, two months before, Walt Gallatin had killed a man — shot him for cutting his barb-wire fence — and that man had been Joe Othon, a Rocking R rider.

Sheriff Rube Bennett had promptly arrested Walt, and introduced him to a cell in the Singletree calaboose. But Walt's uncle was Judge Hamilton Washburn, and this disqualified Judge Washburn from sitting on the trial. Judge Washburn, an old college pal of Judge Bates, had immediately sought the presence of Judge Bates on the Singletree bench, and the two judges had traded jobs for one term of court, Judge Bates to preside in Singletree, Judge Hamilton Washburn to preside in the jurist's old bailiwick, Cowtrail, Territory of Wyoming.

In the two weeks he had been in

Singletree, Judge Bates had learned much, finding that the core of this range war lay in the presence of Val Marcus and his Rocking R. For Marcus ran his Rocking R cows wherever he pleased, on government range and on private property, and, when a man did take up a homestead and fenced it, Marcus or his riders promptly cut the fences, letting Rocking R cattle graze on private property. Thus, in this manner, Val Marcus had run off at least half a score of would-be farmers, and word had gone up and down the railroad that Singletree was no place for a farmer to stop and attempt to practise his trade.

Judge Washburn had told Judge Bates, "Watch out for Sheriff Rube Bennett. Val Marcus elected him sheriff. But you'll find Bennett very ignorant . . . "

And Judge Washburn had made an understatement. Bennett, Tobacco Jones had said, was even more ignorant than their Cowtrail sheriff, Sheriff

Whiting. Judge Bates, though, had disagreed with both his partner and Judge Washburn. He figured that maybe Sheriff Rube Bennett's dumb, peaceful surface was only a blind, and the lawman, although far from brilliant, had a quick mind. As yet, he did not know for sure, though.

Now, hurrying down the alley, listening for the rattle of guns from the Broken Latigo Saloon, the jurist pushed these thoughts aside, for a tough chore lay ahead. A chore he did not relish, but a necessary chore.

For he knew full well the danger in this chore, and never for a moment did he underestimate the danger personified by Val Marcus, by Lew Basick, and by the Rocking R gun-hands. And as he neared the saloon's rear door, he slowed his pace, for he was breathing too heavily, and he wanted to be calm and ready.

His hand was on the latch-string when he heard Val Marcus say sternly, "You goin' some place, Walt?" His belly cold suddenly, the jurist and his sawed-off ten-gauge shotgun slipped inside the saloon.

He came silently, and the men at the front of the long bar were wrapped in their drama and did not see him. The odor of stale whisky, of tobacco smoke, of sawdust, came to him, entering him; he paid it no heed. So far, Tobacco Jones had not entered by the front door, and the judge found himself giving this brief thought, for his partner should have, by all rights, entered the saloon before he had. For Tobacco had been closer to the front door, and the judge had had to go into the alley, get his gun; maybe Tobacco had been held up at the hotel some way.

Walt Gallatin stood on the stairway, facing Val Marcus and Lew Basick. The rider known as Blacky had pushed back his chair and stood, leaning forward a trifle, over the card table, his right hand resting on his leathered six-shooter. Marcus, too, had his hand on his gun; so did Lew Basick. And Judge

Lemanuel Bates, his eyes by this time sharp against the dim light, saw a dull grey color creep across Walt Gallatin's high cheekbones as the young cowman felt the impact of the danger ahead. For the Rocking R had built a deadly and sure trap.

Walt Gallatin had his left hand on the railing, and Judge Bates saw the young cowman's other hand slide and inch backwards toward his pistol.

"A gun trap, eh?" Walt Gallatin's voice was clear, yet it held tightness.

Still, they had not seen Judge Lem Bates. The judge waited, watching, and wondering. Where the devil is Tobacco Jones?

Val Marcus said, "You can call it that, sodbuster. For two months you've been walkin' aroun', free on bail for murderin' one of my riders."

Lew Basick's albino eyes were on Gallatin. They were the cold, unblinking eyes of a reptile. They measured Gallatin and held him. The man called Blacky stood silent, watching, waiting for his cue. Smokey, the owner of the Broken Latigo, had both hands under the bar, and the judge, from where he stood, saw the saloonman had his grip on a shot-gun, hidden from the Rocking R killers.

Smokey said dangerously, "Don't go through with this, Marcus!"

Marcus never took his gaze off Walt Gallatin. From the corner of his mouth he said quickly, "Watch this barman, Blacky. And when the guns roar, kill him. We don't want no witnesses around."

"I'll get one or two before you kill me," Smokey growled.

Judge Bates saw, then and there, that he and Gallatin had an ally in the scrappy saloonman. And when Tobacco Jones came in —

Marcus was speaking again, talking in a slow voice, never hurried, never blustering.

"This is sewed up tight as a drum," Marcus stated. "When this is over, Gallatin, you'll be dead, an' so will

Smokey. When we get on the witness stand — before your good friend Judge Bates — me an' my hands'll swear you picked a fight with me and I killed you in self-defense. And who will there be to state otherwise?"

The jurist could wait no longer for his partner. He said clearly, "Judge Lem Bates will state otherwise, Marcus!"

Blacky turned — a jerky movement, yet swift — and he had his gun half-drawn. Then he looked squarely into the muzzle of Judge Lem Bates' scatter-gun and drew his hand back, something seeping into his dark features and taking color away. Lew Basick, too, pivoted, studied the shotgun, lifted his pale eyes upward, meeting Judge Bates' gaze. And the half-smile around the big mouth of Judge Lem Bates made Lew Basick's thin lips lose their derision.

Val Marcus darted a glance at Judge Bates, then pulled his gaze back to Gallatin, still on the stairway. Smokey said, "Thanks, Judge."

Gallatin said suddenly, "You saved my life, Bates."

Judge Bates said, "Walk to that door, Gallatin, and go to my office." Then, to the Rocking R cowboys, "Don't any of you pull a gun. Did you ever see a stiff who got shot with a sawed-off ten-gauge at this close distance? He'd have a hole in him big enough to drive a four-horse team through."

Blacky glanced at Marcus. Lew Basick's dead eyes shuttled toward the Rocking R boss. Silence for a thin second, and then Marcus said, "They've got us, this time. But there'll be another."

Gallatin came gingerly down the steps, hand on his gun, walking as though he trod on ground glass. He reached the end of the stairs and backed toward the door, crouched and watchful. He said, "Thanks, Bates," and backed into somebody who was just entering. He pivoted, gun rising; then he held his weapon unfired, the barrel straight and demanding.

"This is a rough town," a voice said.

Judge Bates had expected Tobacco Jones to enter, but the speaker was a woman — thick of thigh and bosom, a little hat perched on her head, the plume arching down over her back. The blackness of her silk dress glistened with an ebony darkness. Walt Gallatin had bumped into her large stomach.

Gallatin said roughly, "There's danger here, madam; get out of my way. Get out!"

"I've never been thrown out of a saloon in my life, young man, and I'm too young to pick up such a precarious habit here. If you want to leave, step around me, sir!"

Judge Bates smiled, but kept his eyes on Marcus and Basick, after noticing that Smokey had his scatter-gun lying over the bar, but pointing toward Blacky. Gallatin squeezed around her, for she almost filled the doorway, and disappeared up the street.

The woman stopped, looking at the men, judging their weapons. "I did

24

indeed step into a wild party," she finally said. She moved forward, silk crinkling, and rested one of her high-laced shoes on the polished brass of the bar rail. "All right, boys, have your fun. But while you enjoy yourself, would the bartender please serve me with a shot of Tom Watson?"

"Not now," Smokey said.

The woman said, "Well, pleasure before business, then." She looked at Judge Lem Bates, and the jurist noticed the full smile around her wide mouth. "But, sir, I do not believe your friends here will fight. They looked cowed to me."

"Who the blazes are you?" Val Marcus wanted to know.

"Your courtesy, sir, has seemingly been forgotten," the woman said.

Judge Bates moved forward. "You are right, madam," he assured her. "Mr. Marcus seems to have lost his courtesy, also his sense of fair play. Smokey, cover this bunch, while I talk to Marcus."

"With pleasure Judge Bates."

The woman's heavy brows lifted. "*The* Judge Lemanuel Bates, sir?"

"Reckon I'm him, madam."

Val Marcus looked at the jurist's shot-gun. Then he looked full at Judge Bates. "What's runnin' through your mind, Bates? Surely you, a judge sworn to uphold the law, won't murder a man by shootin' him through the belly?" He appeared unworried and unruffled and for the first time Judge Lem Bates really got an insight into the man's toughness.

"No, not that, Marcus."

The jurist's shotgun lifted, hard and fast, then came down quickly. Val Marcus tried to duck, but the barrel hit him across the left side of his head, ripping his Stetson from his hair. The blow spilled him onto the floor, where he sat dazed and bloody.

Lew Basick had moved toward Judge Bates, and Smokey's shotgun suddenly jammed into the range boss' back. "Be nice," Smokey warned.

Basick stopped, tense, white eyebrows low, the jauntiness leaving him, seeping his strength from him.

Basick said, "You got all the cards, Smokey."

Judge Bates stooped, got Marcus' gun, took Basick's pistol, then crossed the room to disarm Blacky.

Blacky warned, "Don't keep that gun of mine, Bates. I've had that a long, long time."

The judge assured the gunman that, after he and Basick and Marcus had thought this over and regained their right senses — if they ever did reach such a state — they could have their guns back, for he would deposit them in Sheriff Rube Bennett's office.

"You'd better get it back to me," Blacky warned.

The jurist's shotgun rose again and again swiftly descended. Blacky yowled, grabbed for his head, and fell back into the chair, sobbing in pain and anger. Judge Bates, smiling a little, spoke to Lew Basick.

"There is a gentleman around this town, Basick, whom I've heard you call 'an old moocher.' Not more than fifteen minutes ago he sat at a card table here and you men chased him out."

"You mean that tall shoe-button, the one that always chews Horseshoe eatin' tobaccer?"

"That is he."

"What about him?"

"He was stationed here to watch out for the safety of young Gallatin. He came and told me of your trap here. That old bum, sir, is my partner, Tobacco Jones."

"You didn't ride into town together," Val Marcus declared.

The judge assured him that was true. "We wanted to scout the lay of things first, Marcus. From now on, we act together, you may be assured."

"You're marked," Basick growled.

Val Marcus got slowly to his feet, rubbing his head gingerly. He pulled his hand down and looked at it. "Don't tip your hand, Basick," he growled angrily. "Blacky, get on your boots, and get out of here."

Blacky got up, spat at Judge Bates, but his aim was poor and he missed, almost hitting the strange, heavy-set woman. He lurched out the door, Basick following him, with Val Marcus trailing. They crossed the street to their tied broncs, and there Jim Crow joined them.

The judge noticed that Jim Crow's shirt was torn and his nose was swollen as though fists had worked him over. He also noticed that Jim Crow, upon mounting his bronc, swung up slowly, as though he were stiff in the joints. Dust covered the back of Crow's torn shirt and pants, and the judge figured he had been rolled in the street dust.

"Somebody must've beat him up, too."

A voice said, "I whupped the son, Bates."

3

TOBACCO JONES stood in the doorway, a twisted smile on his homely mouth, his upper lip puffed and still swelling, his shirt in ribbons. The man's skinny chest, the judge noticed, bore the marks of hard fists, these marks red against the paleness of his skin.

"What happened, Tobacco?"

Tobacco Jones informed him that, as he hurried toward the Broken Latigo Saloon, Jim Crow, stationed across the street, had jumped him, warning him to stay out of the saloon.

"So I hit him, Bates. He knocked me down first, an' thet got me right mad."

"Only dogs get *mad*," the judge corrected him.

Tobacco studied him coldly, his good eye metallic and stern, the other rapidly swelling shut. "All right, Bates, I got hot under the saddle blanket, if'n you like that better. I tied into him then in earnest, and I guess I cleaned his clock for him, eh?" The Cowtrail postmaster looked at the heavy-set woman. "Howdy, ma'am. How's your instep?"

"It is a little swollen, sir."

"Right sorry to hear that, ma'am. That suitcase was right heavy, too. You left it at the hotel, I noticed."

Judge Bates listened in puzzled wonder. "Tobacco," he asked, "have you advertised for a wife, and is this lady she?"

Tobacco Jones got very red. He almost swallowed his chew. The woman laughed and told the jurist about meeting his partner and colliding with him. "I dropped my suitcase, Judge, and it landed on my instep; it was full of lead."

"Lead?"

"Yes, printer's lead."

"I'll never git married," Tobacco

assured her. "I ain't the marryin' kind, I tell you."

"Me, I've been hooked double four times," the woman stated. "We always got to kicking at each other across the wagon-pole, and I finally kicked myself out of each set of tugs." A dreamy look entered her big, ox-like eyes. "But that don't say I wouldn't try it again."

"Don't look at me," Tobacco said smiling. "The judge is single, too."

The jurist, never one to fall down on the ladies, introduced his partner formally, stressing the fact that Tobacco Jones, too, was a public man; when not fist-fighting, and when at home, he was Cowtrail's postmaster. He then introduced Smokey and in turn introduced himself, although the latter was, of course, absolutely unnecessary.

"I'm Margaret Shaw," the woman informed them. "Friends call me Maggie; enemies call me a devil in petticoats. I am a printer, men; a wandering, foot-loose newspaperwoman, and I intend to start a weekly periodical in this village.

My press is due today or tomorrow on the local freight. And now, Friend Smokey, that slug of Tom Watson I ordered. You will drink with me, Judge, and you too, Mr. Jones."

"Tobacco doesn't drink, Maggie," the judge supplied.

Maggie Shaw looked long and startled at the jurist. "Surely, Judge Bates, you are fabricating? For what would a man's life be — or a woman's, either — were it not for an occasional sip at the flowing bowl."

"I hate the smell of the stuff," Tobacco growled.

Maggie Shaw shook her thick head, apparently not understanding such a quirk in a human's character. Smokey dexterously fixed the drinks and took a jigger himself. "To more and better fights," he toasted.

The jurist tossed his liquor down the hatch, glancing at Maggie Shaw, who drank like a veteran, even disdaining water for a chaser, and the whisky was wild and strong. She smacked her lips and poured another drink. "You will soon find, Smokey, that I am one of your best customers."

"My trade picked up when Bates here came to town," the bartender beamed. "He buys it by the jug."

"Cheaper that way, Maggie."

Tobacco asked, "I reckon Marcus an' his snakes wiggled their way out of town, eh, Bates?"

The judge thought that perhaps Marcus had stopped to have a word with Sheriff Rube Bennett. "He won't want Bennett to hear our side of the story first, Jones. So he'll stop an' blah with him."

Tobacco scowled, then. He said, "And young Walt Gallatin went to your office, didn't he? Maybe I'd better sashay up there an' keep an eye on things. Me, I sure ain't got no use to be in this vilesmelling saloon." He stopped at the door. "There rides out Marcus an' his bullsnakes now. Sure 'nough, Bates, he stopped and talked with Bennett, I'll betcha."

"Go get young Walt down here."

Tobacco spat into the dust, then hurried through the falling twilight. The judge, having a new drinking pal, set up the drinks, and let Maggie do the talking. A true newshound, she started questioning him about Val Marcus, asked why he wanted to kill Walt Gallatin; when the judge told her the background of the case — how Walt, seemingly in self-defense, had killed Joe Othon, the Rocking R rider, and how he had come to sit on the local bench, because kinship with Walt Gallatin had disqualified the local jurist, Judge Washburn — the woman's eyes glowed with an interest not all prompted by the alcohol she had absorbed.

"This is just what I am looking for, Judge Bates. I tell you, sir, I arrived at the right place at the correct time. Why, even now I feel an editorial coming on — one blasting Marcus and his Rocking R crew for holding up the progress of Singletree town by

35

keeping farmers from plowing up these virgin fields."

The judge advised her not to jump at conclusions but to look around carefully before launching into an editorial tirade. This angered Maggie, who reminded him he perhaps knew more about law than she, but did he know anything about newspapers?

"I never argue with a woman, Mrs. Shaw."

"That right? You must live a dull life, Judge. And what is more, Val Marcus won't argue with me, either."

A buckboard, pulled by two sorrels, came down the street, dust lifting under its iron-rimmed wheels. The judge saw that a woman held the reins, and a little girl of about three sat on the leather-covered high seat beside her. The sorrels were tired, sweat rimmed against their shoulders back of the collars, and they jogged along, their energies spent.

"Mrs. Gallatin," Smokey said.

The judge regarded Sarah Gallatin,

looking over his whisky glass. She was a small woman, young and fresh with youth's power, and he liked the set of her square small shoulders, the loveliness of her blonde, pretty head. "And little Matilda," he added.

"Prob'ly worried about her husband," Smokey supplied.

The woman and child and rig moved out of sight beyond the edge of the window, but Judge Bates heard her halt the team in front of the hotel. Maggie said that Matilda was a terrible name, in her estimation, to put on a child, and the jurist, deep in sudden musings, remarked that it could scarcely be worse than Maggie as a name, and at this, instead of becoming incensed, Maggie Shaw laughed deeply and wished the judge had been present at her birth. "I hate the name too, Bates, but my mother put it on me. Wish you'd have been there to talk her out of it."

"Yes, and if I had, I'd been so old I'd been dead now."

At this, Maggie's heavy shoulders

took on a hurt tilt and she reminded him she wasn't so old that men still didn't propose to her. The jurist said she would never catch him proposing matrimony to her and then, in the nick of time, caught his words and held them, winking at Smokey and saying, "Funny thing about a woman, friend. There is little a man can say that they do not take offense at."

"They sure got that habit, Bates."

Maggie let that remark ride, resuming her rapid questioning of the jurist and the bartender. "A newspaperwomen has to keep on the alert," she informed them. "She has to keep asking questions and prying into other peoples' affairs."

"A newspaper reporter," the judge said solemnly, "is, in my opinion, nothing but a nuisance. They are spies, nothing more."

Again Maggie did not rise to the bait. She slapped the bar and said loudly, "Thanks, Your Honor. You have unwittingly named my paper. *The Singletree Spy*. How does that sound?"

"It has alliteration, if nothing else," the jurist said.

Maggie paid her bill with, "And now to go out and hire an office. Is there a vacant building in town, something not too big or expensive, but a substantial building, one that can hold a press and my supplies?"

Judge Bates reminded her that he was a comparative newcomer to Singletree. Smokey scowled and rubbed his jaw slowly. Finally he said that the building across the street was empty. An undertaker had a shop there for a year, but nobody had paid him any attention, and he had loaded up his coffins and drifted on.

"Nobody ever die here?" Maggie wanted to know.

Smokey reminded her that death was inevitable, talking in a low, solemn tone. No, the undertaker's prices had been so high people had built their own rough-boxes, and had done their own burying. "A undertaker is only a human vulture," the saloon keeper soliloquized, "that lives off the tears and misfortunes of the bereaved."

"Something like a newspaper reporter, eh, Bates?"

Again, the judge had no answer; his mind was not on jesting. Maggie streamed out the door, leaving a faint odor of perfume behind her. The door went shut and her shoes, slapping hard on the plank sidewalk, lost their rap-rap in the distance. Smokey wiped the bar slowly.

"Thinking of Walt Gallatin, Your Honor?"

The judge nodded. Walt Gallatin, he said, was in great danger. By staging this gun trap, Val Marcus and Lew Basick had openly defied the law, and this defiance, to him, had assumed the character of an open taunt, a flagrant disregard for the law and the bench he represented.

"Marcus is tough, Judge. He's had things his own way in the time he's spent here." Smokey wrung out his bar towel over a bucket. "He wants all this range for his cows, an' he'll fight to hold it, in court and out. With you being a friend of Judge Washburn's, I kinda figure he thinks Walt Gallatin will get acquitted, for sure. So he took it on himself to get rid of Walt."

"Poor range to die for," the judge stated.

Smokey resumed his wiping of the bar, attacking a spot that marred the varnish. "I've thought that, too, sir. But if water were put on this land, Bates, it would bloom like the Garden of Eden. And I understand Walt Gallatin is shippin' in a well-drillin' outfit to dig for water."

The judge reminded him that the Garden of Eden, to the best of his knowledge, never had had any snow on it; snow banked high here during the winter. But this was a small point, he allowed, and was merely a vagrant thought. Yes, with deep wells kicking out good water to run into irrigation ditches, Broken Creek, the side of Gallatin's homestead, would really raise

41

alfafa and grain. But surely Val Marcus knew this fact; why didn't he in turn, dig wells?

"He's a cowman, Judge, first, last, and always. He wants range to run on and he cuts hay in the draws for winter feeding. His mind is made up, I figure, and only death will change it."

"Any way you look at it, then, sir, it spells *trouble* with *capital* letters?"

Smokey wrung out his towel again and again attacked the blemish in the varnish. From now on out, Marcus would be his enemy, but that, he said, did not bother him, even though he would lose the Rocking R trade.

"Always the almighty dollar hooked up with it, Smokey. Well, I'm going upstairs and talk with John Wimberley."

4

HE was a tall man, around six feet three, and because of his great gaunt height, he had a hard time getting suits to fit him. Now he dozed in his chair, feet on his desk, his eyes lidded with thin, dark lids that had dark bags like half-moons suspended below them.

Judge Bates said, "Mr. Wimberley?"

The eyelids opened, showing the eyes above the dark bags, and the polished boots came down to the floor. The thin moustache over the upper lip lifted and a smile presumably meant to be pleasant touched the sunken cheeks with the black roots of shaven whiskers.

"Judge Lemanuel Bates, sir! This is indeed an honor." John Wimberley rose to his gaunt height, his blue suit falling in folds around his thin person.

A bony hand designated a leather-backed chair. "You will be seated, sir?"

Judge Bates took the proffered chair, slumping in it as usual. John Wimberley, his welcoming task completed, sent his sparse frame downward until it met his chair, and leaned his pointed elbows on his desk, building a pyramid with his fingers. He looked over this pyramid at the heavy-set jurist.

"You come for a pleasure visit, Judge Bates, or do you come for business?"

The judge had to admit to himself that Lawyer John Wimberley went straight to the point. "On what side do you stand in this trouble, sir?"

The long fingers bent, moving the apex of the pyramid up and down, and finally they steadied, the peak of the pyramid sharp and hard. "You are blunt, sir, and I suppose you demand a blunt answer?" Wimberley did not wait for confirmation. "I am hired by retainer fee to represent young Walt Gallatin, Your Honor."

The judge realized, with a little smile, that Wimberley had told him nothing concrete but had climbed on the middle of the fence skilfully. This man, he knew, had a sharp, keen mind, trained to quick thinking and quick retort, yet well versed in the loopholes of the law and ever ready to utilize these loopholes.

This uncanny ability to circumvent the law had, in a small degree, given John Wimberley a slight tainted reputation among men of the bench and bar, and Judge Lem Bates was remembering this. He had inquired about Wimberley and had found out that the lawyer had only come to Singletree the year before. He had pondered on this fact, for it seemed odd, at that time, that Wimberley, with his legal prowess, would settle in a town so small and with so little trade as this Wyoming territorial cow-town. For some strange reason this puzzle had bothered him.

Accordingly, he reminded Wimberley

that, but a few minutes before, Val
Marcus and Lew Basick had, downstairs,
set a gun trap for young Walt Gallatin.
He told how he, with the aid of
Smokey, had broken up the plot to
murder the rancher. At this, John
Wimberley's eyes, instead of rising in
surprise, became lidded a moment, as
though the lawyer were giving this
information deep and brief thought.

"I heard no sound of the ruckus,
Judge Bates." A hand flew out, breaking
up the pyramid, then settled back, the
fingernails long and polished. "But
the floors are thick, Your Honor;
perhaps they muffled the sounds.
And besides, I settled myself for a
little nap the minute the door closed
behind Walt."

That sounded logical, the jurist
mentally agreed. He asked, in a
round-about way, if, in Wimberley's
opinion, Val Marcus had much of a
case against Walt Gallatin, and to this
Wimberley replied that, in his humble
opinion, Marcus had no case at all

that would stand up under the legal spotlight.

"I understand that Marcus has no witnesses to the fatal gunfight, Your Honor. My client has his wife for witness and also his hired man, old Jim Potter. They will get on the witness stand and testify that Joe Othon threatened my client, and then drew his gun against him, making my client shoot in self-defense. But come, Your Honor, we are not supposed to discuss the case before the trial gets into action."

The judge agreed, according to law, that Wimberley was correct, yet the law was not always followed to the letter. He wondered why the county attorney had even issued a warrant for Walt Gallatin's arrest on such flimsy evidence.

"Perhaps if you talk to him, Judge Bates, he will drop the charge?"

The judge assured him he would talk to the man. He got to his feet, suddenly wishing he had a drink, yet not wanting to ask Wimberley if he had a bottle in his desk. His visit had brought no conclusion other than that Wimberley was a smooth character.

Wimberley stroked his moustache, and was silent. The judge, took his departure, walking slowly down the stairway on which, but a few minutes before, Walt Gallatin had faced death. From outside came the wail of a violin — a screeching, off-key wail that brought a grimace to the judge's wide mouth. Evidently the noise came from the sidewalk outside.

Smokey stood behind the bar, rag still on the varnish, listening with open mouth to the wail. Walt Gallatin and Tobacco Jones stood on the customer side of the bar, both looking toward the window. Judge Bates stopped and also looked at the window.

"Somebody must be gettin' killed," Tobacco ventured.

"Either that," Gallatin said, "or he's got the D.T.'s."

Now a figure moved into the glass

square, and they saw the player. He was short and of indeterminate age, his violin pushed under his bony jaw, his bow rising and falling. He wore smoked glasses and his gait was the slow, uncertain gait of a blind man. A faded red coat, trimmed with braid that had been once a violent yellow, covered his narrow, peaked shoulders, and a wide-brimmed flat hat, black with a faded band, sat on the back of his head, showing dark, sparse hair on a flat skull. A monkey crouched on his left shoulder — the one nearest the window.

He was a small monkey with a long, curling tail, the end of it not being visible because of the window's smallness. The monkey had a pinched, sad face and Judge Bates, watching and wondering, found a striking resemblance between the features of the monkey and the violin player.

The monkey turned bright shoe-button eyes on them, evidently seeing them despite the dirty window-pane, and then the violinist and monkey moved out of the square. The high-pitched wail went past the door and gradually lost power as the violinist went down the street.

"Now who t'Hades is he?" Smokey marveled.

"Probably a wandering blind man," the jurist said, coming to the bar. "What was that piece he was playing, Tobacco?"

"Was that *music*, Judge?"

By this time distance had stilled the violin. Judge Lemanuel Bates gave his attention to more pressing matters. He scolded Walt Gallatin roundly, using the tone of a father bawling out a son.

"You should never ride alone, sir. Always have a hired hand with you, for by this time you should realize your life is in danger."

Gallatin took the scolding, his young face solemn with thought. He agreed that the jurist was correct, but he had only one hired hand and that was old

Jim Potter. The judge had seen Jim Potter once or twice — an ancient, broken-down cowhand — but yet, he told the rancher, Jim Potter had eyes to see with.

"You have a splendid young wife, sir, and a wonderful little daughter. For their sake, if not for your own, do not expose yourself to danger again."

"Heck of a country where a man has to ride with a friend to watch his backtrail!" Anger twisted the rancher's face into hard lines. "Where is this sheriff of ours, the one we pay a good salary to?"

"Asleep in his office," Tobacco growled.

"I left Jim at home to guard the ranch," Gallatin informed them. "I have to hire another hand, I reckon. But where can a man get a reliable rider, men? They work until they get a whiskey stake, then draw their time and skip out to the nearest saloon. Whiskey is a tough master, sirs."

The jurist corrected, "Whiskey is no

master of a good man, Walt. Whiskey is only the boss of the mentally sick and the weak. To a man who has a good perspective on life, hard liquor is only a slight stimulant, nothing more."

"You should know, Bates." Tobacco Jones, despite his swollen upper lip, smiled dryly.

That remark broke up the tension, but still underneath lay the grim, raw threat of trouble — a spectre stalking this range of mountains and valleys and creeks. They all drank — except Tobacco — and the jurist told Gallatin to come with him to Sheriff Rube Bennett's office, where he would demand protection for the Gallatin family and holdings.

"I tell you, Bennett ain't no good, Bates. He'll grin and smile and mumble something. He jus' draws his wages easy, an' let's it go at that."

The judge reminded him that he was Bennett's superior and that the sheriff would have to obey his orders. Gallatin said that his uncle, Judge Washburn, had tried to dictate to Bennett, but had gotten nowhere.

Tobacco Jones cut in with, "Rube Bennett doesn't know Judge Bates, Walt. When the judge hollers, Bennett better leave that chair in a hurry, if he's got any brains. And if he doesn't leave it, the judge will see he moves right pronto."

"Thanks, Tobacco."

The stairs creaked, and Lawyer Wimberley came down, walking slowly. He smiled and offered to buy the drinks, but the judge, for once, turned down a free drink. He explained to Wimberley that he was going to demand that Bennett protect Walt Gallatin and his holdings. At this Wimberley nodded slowly, stroked his small moustache, and hoped that Judge Bates would have more power over Rube Bennett than had Judge Washburn. Bennett, he said, had a mind of his own, and figured he ran the county attorney and county judge.

"I shall soon change his mind,"

Judge Lemanuel Bates said. And he added, as an afterthought. "And when I change it, it will stay changed, sir."

Wimberley kept stroking his moustache. Tobacco Jones, seeing an amused smile touch the lawyer's lips very faintly, felt a touch of anger — evidently Wimberley figured his partner was boasting. Had Wimberley known the judge as well as he knew him, he wouldn't have smiled. Tobacco bit off a chew and decided to keep silent.

"Legally, Bennett should provide a deputy for Gallatin's protection," Wimberley said. He drank alone, tossing his whiskey down with a quick, short gesture. Then he drank deeply of the water used for a chaser. "Smokey, what do you put in that stuff? Strychnine?"

"We had a woman in here that drank it without water," Smokey informed him. He told the lawyer about Maggie Shaw and her proposed news-sheet, *The Singletree Spy*. Wimberley's long fingers played with his glass. "Another nuisance, huh? As if we don't have enough trouble." The sounds of the violin became stronger. "Now who in heaven's name is that blind gent?"

Nobody knew, of course.

They listened to the violin come closer. And the judge, always one with an ear for music in any form, found himself trying to determine what piece the violinist was playing. Once he thought he had a clue and then a discordant note came in, breaking up the melody, and he decided the violinist was a poor player, indeed.

Again the man passed, walking with the uncertain gait of a blind man in strange surroundings, and again the monkey peered in the window, ugly face wrinkled, eyes shrewd and warm. A bunch of town kids followed the player this time, shouting and laughing, and then they were gone. But the noise, instead of retreating, found an even, distant pitch.

"Oh, fine!" Smokey growled. "He's

stationed himself at the corner. He'll drive what little trade I have got out of the country!"

"Here comes Walt's wife," Tobacco said.

5

SHERIFF RUBE BENNETT dozed, boots resting on his desk, his spur rowels gouging through the varnish and digging holes in the walnut top. He had drifted into Singletree a few years before, poor as a church-mouse, and had begun punching cows for the Rocking R. He had married the undertaker's daughter and she, each spring since then, had regularly presented him with a child. People said he slept days in his office because he never got any sleep at home at nights.

The undertaker, because of his profession, had also been county coroner, and he, not wanting his daughter and her increasing brood to face starvation, got Rube into politics, getting him a position as deputy to old Harry Landon, the sheriff who had retired, term before last, because of old age. The undertaker had left town, but Rube Bennett continued his well-paying ride on the political lumber-wagon. He'd run for sheriff and, to his surprise, had been elected.

A range bum a few years ago, he was now sheriff; this had gone to his head. He knew full well that Val Marcus and the Rocking R had been instrumental in getting him elected, but, as yet, Marcus has not openly demanded his repayment for swinging the votes of the Rocking R riders in his direction. Many times Rube Bennett wondered what Marcus would demand in repayment. For the election had been very close, only the votes of Rocking R riders swinging it in favor of Bennett.

Well, he had the job now; let Marcus make demands. The power of the star had gone like a heady wine to Sheriff Rube Bennett's skull. Never a brainy man at his best, he had managed to get through the fifth grade but, at that grade, he had had a fight with his male teacher, for the teacher had ordered him to go home and shave. Rube Bennett had claimed he had shaved that morning. The teacher, angered now, had said he was lying, and it became a matter of personalities rather than of issues. So Rube Bennett had trounced the teacher and quit school to drift west.

Never one to be stirred by the innate pride that comes with leadership of men and community affairs, after election he became very much the leader and, to a degree, an overbearing individual. When he had bummed credit in the local saloons, had his cigarette lain on the bar and burned through the varnish he would have apologized profusely for his unthoughtfulness and the damage it had created. He would have, in fact, offered to pay for his damages. Now, with a star on his coat, with a few extra nickels in his pockets, he was just the opposite; neither property or individuals meant much to him.

Not that he was innately mean or

ugly. No, he had been the bottom dog all his life, he had had the pack run over him and tear at him; now he was, in his estimation, on the top; he would use his fangs in retaliation. He had worked his way up, hadn't he?

He knew that all his good luck — and his bad luck — had come when he had married the undertaker's daughter, yet he had lied to himself so much that, because of constant repetition, he had got to the point where he believed his own fabrications. Day by day his ego grew in direct proportion to the days he had spent in his new capacity as law administrator to this territorial county.

He gouged his right spur deeper into the desk, scraping off whatever varnish remained, and he rolled the sharp rowel deeper into the walnut, scowling and wondering why he didn't go home. He knew why. The kids would be bawling, as usual, and his wife's tongue would be razor-sharp, as usual. He'd stay in his office a while longer to make sure the kids were in bed, then he'd grab some chuck at the Longhorn, and would try to make home by the back door, for there might be a chance to sneak in that way.

His wife, smarter than he, had never fallen for the power of his star; she was the boss, intended to remain the boss, and she had told him, more times than he could remember, that no little piece of polished metal would make her quit bossing him, even if that metal were pounded out to become a five-pointed star.

Deep in his thoughts, he was dully aware that boots were coming down the courthouse hall, pounding as boots can pound against concrete. Whoever owned those boots — and it sounded like two men — also evidently owned a key to the front door, for office hours were over and the janitor was sweeping up the joint. Maybe it was the county assessor coming back to work nights, his assistant with him, for tax bills would be mailed out soon. He had asked the assessor once to raise taxes, thereby figuring he might get a larger salary, but the man had told him this was the job of the county commissioners, not the duty of his office. This had not set well, for some reason, and he figured, with his ignorance of the law, that the assessor was giving him the run-around and did really have the power to raise the tax rate. At any rate, he could raise the assessed valuation, and thereby take in more tax revenue.

He hoped the assessor and his clerk would pass without speaking or entering, but he heard the boots behind him enter the office; still he did not look up, but pretended he was dozing.

"Sheriff Bennett, Judge Bates and Mr. Jones."

Bennett spoke without dropping his feet or turning his head. "Come in," he said. "Take chairs, men."

Frankly, he had not yet catalogued Judge Bates, nor his partner, either.

Judge Washburn had been an old, tolerant jurist, who, when the object of demands, had smiled, said he would look into the matter, and, as far back as Sheriff Bennett could remember, never gave either a direct no or yes, but was content to ride the stream.

But Judge Bates, in the few days he had held down the local bench, had proved to be the opposite of Judge Washburn; he made decisions — quick decisions — and held to them. Sheriff Bennett, who knew, although he would not admit it, that he was running more or less on bluff, had found no satisfaction in the judge's presence.

"You wish to talk about some legal problem, Judge Bates?"

Judge Bates had settled in an arm chair, and Sheriff Bennett, noting the whisky jug beside the jurist, scowled a little. He had completely misjudged the heavy-set jurist. He figured that Judge Lemanuel Bates was a confirmed drunkard, one who could not get out of sight of this jug. He used this as a key to a weakness in the jurist's character: the judge, he figured, didn't have much gumption, or why would he take a jug with him all the time?

And here, on this single point, Sheriff Rube Bennett had made a mistake, a serious mistake.

Although Judge Bates drank, he never drank to excess. Had Bennett ever questioned Tobacco Jones he would have found out two things: Judge Bates could quit drinking whenever he so made up his mind and, no matter how much he drank, he never became intoxicated. As it was, Bennett felt it was indeed poor taste for a man of the bench to tote around a jug of raw whisky; it did not, Bennett thought, fit the dignity of the job.

"Val Marcus tried to gun down young Walt Gallatin," Tobacco Jones said.

When Bennett had been a rounder in the local saloons, such stirring news would have filled him with rapid questions. But now, a man of the star, he forced his face to be calm, his gaze to be blank and dull.

"Are you sure of that, Mr. Jones?"

Tobacco jammed his cud into his cheek, eyes getting hard. "I can see, Bennett," he said.

Bennett saw Judge Bates grin. The jurist then told about the attempted killing in the Broken Latigo. Bennett listened, then asked, "Why didn't you notify me, Jones, instead of Judge Bates? I carry the star here, sir. And you could have told me, too; you bumped into me in the hall."

"Never figgered you'd do nothin', Bennett."

Bennett felt anger but hoped he hid it. Judge Bates told him that Marcus and his Rocking R men had left town. Bennett asked if he, the judge, wanted a warrant issued for their arrest. At this, anger ran through the corpulent jurist.

"Sir, Marcus stopped in here, and, unless I am mistaken, he wanted you to issue a warrant for my arrest. But to get it in legal action, I would have to sign that warrant. Is that not right?"

Bennett just looked at him.

"We saw Marcus come in here," Tobacco Jones supplied.

Bennett admitted Marcus had called on him. This knowledge still further angered Judge Bates and, had Bennett known the jurist well, he would have read these signs of anger and drawn back his horns. But this, he figured, was the showdown; he'd bossed Judge Washburn — or so he'd thought — and he'd have a showdown now with this new upstart judge.

"Had Marcus grounds for a warrant against you, Bates, I'd've issued one, sir. But I thought his evidence was danged weak."

"You couldn't issue a warrant, Sheriff Bennett."

"I'm the law in this county, Judge."

Judge Bates got to his feet. "No warrant can be legal unless it has my signature, Bennett. You may be elected sheriff but, for the present, I am judge of this county, and your superior." The judge caught his temper. "Now, as judge, I demand you send a deputy out to the Gallatin ranch, there to post himself as a guard over Gallatin's property."

Bennett studied the jurist. He was losing his arrogance, for Judge Washburn had never talked in this commanding tone to him, and he hoped he kept this from showing. He made a pretense at being angry.

"Why should the taxpayers stand the bill of a deputy sittin' aroun' out at Gallatin's?"

The judge reminded him that Walt Gallatin was out on bail on a murder charge and therefore it was up to the county to defend and protect him until his court trial.

Bennett shook his head. "Don't think a deputy is necessary," he said stubbornly.

The judge pounded on the corner of the desk with balled fist. "Sheriff Bennett, this is a direct insubordination!

I order you to get a deputy to the Gallatin ranch; you refuse. Unless you do so, I hereby order your office vacated, and shall, in the morning, choose a successor to hold your office until such time as an election can be called to elect a true representative of the people."

Bennett studied him. "You can't do that, Your Honor."

"Your knowledge of the law, sir, if I may say so, is very scanty. I ask you, before going further, to go into the county attorney's office — or into my office, sir — and look up Code Number 19 and 20 of Section Five of the Civil and Executive Section, Territory of Wyoming, and you will find the section devoted to just such insubordination as you present here. The volume number, sir, is 9."

Bennett said, "All right, Bates. I'll send a deputy out tonight. I'll give him orders to stay on the job until you tell him his work is over."

Judge Bates smiled. "Drink, sir?"

"Not now. Too close to supper."

The jurist corked his jug. "I am indeed sorry I had to talk this way, sir. I will demand utmost co-operation from your office on this case or any other case we encounter, and you may be sure my co-operation will be yours, too."

Tobacco, unnoticed by Bennett, winked long and slowly at the judge.

"Then a deputy will ride out to Gallatin's immediately?" the jurist asked.

Bennett assured him that would be done. "But, sir," and he raised a bony hand, "I shall consult the county attorney in the morning, and in this way I'll know where I stand, Bates."

Again, anger colored the judge's thick jowls. But Tobacco Jones, standing behind Sheriff Bennett, shook his long head slowly, and the judge, taking his partner's advice, decided to skip the matter.

"You have that privilege, sir."

The partners went outside into the hall, intending to go to the hotel and play some pitch or whist, for already they had made the acquaintance of two old fellows who were pensioners there. Tobacco grumbled. "That big-mouthed pup, Bates! Did you see how them rowels of his'n were rippin' up that desk? Why, he ain't even got no respect for county prop'rty!"

"I'd sure've liked to jerk that chair out from under his fat beam," the jurist growled.

Somebody was rattling the front door. The jurist slipped the lock, and a small man stood in the dim light of the street lamp. It was the blind violinist, his monkey still on his shoulder.

"This is no saloon," Tobacco Jones said. "This is the county courthouse, fella."

The man had a low, deep voice that seemed out of place in his thin neck. "It is the courthouse I search for, sirs. I look for your local sheriff who, I am led to understand, is named Rube Bennett."

70

The monkey jumped on the jurist's shoulder. Judge Bates not knowing what to do, stood silent. The monkey ran one paw slowly across the judge's wide face, evidently seemed to like him, and put his hairy arms around the judge's neck. The judge felt the moist imprint of the monkey's lips on his cheek. The whiskers were sharp as wires, though.

"Alexander, where did you go?"

"He's on my shoulder, sir," the judge answered.

The blind man tugged on the leash, but Alexander, seemingly loath to leave Judge Bates, hugged the jurist harder, chattering softly. Judge Bates stroked the wiry, small body with its coarse hair.

"He likes me, sir."

"That is odd, sir. Usually Alexander is everybody's enemy. What is your name, sir?"

"Judge Lemanuel Bates. And this is my partner, Tobacco Jones."

"I have heard of you, Judge Bates.

But you are out of your bailiwick, are you not? I am led to believe this is Singletree, not Cowtrail."

"You are a traveler, sir?"

The man introduced himself as Ponce de Leon Smith. His father, he said, had been a Spaniard with a great admiration for Ponce de Leon. His grandfather, he related, had been named Smith. It got rather complicated, or so Tobacco Jones thought.

"I understand, Judge Bates, that in order to ply my trade — some people refer to me as a peddler, you know — I must procure first a license to sell my wares, here in Singletree?"

The judge told him that no such state or county statute existed, but perhaps the Singletree town council had made up such an ordinance. If they had, it was in direct violation of the territorial code. Nevertheless, perhaps it would be best to consult Sheriff Bennett, for the county attorney was, at the moment, out of town, and besides, it was after office hours for the county attorney.

They went down the corridor, Ponce de Leon Smith in the middle, cane rapping on the concrete. Tobacco Jones was on the blind man's left with Judge Bates, monkey still on his shoulder, on Smith's right.

"A new environment," Smith said, "is hard on a blind man, sirs. In old surroundings he knows his way about, for sudden air currents coming around buildings tell him his whereabouts, as do currents coming from open doors and windows. And he can also keep a count of his paces, too. But, alas, in a new town — "

"You do well, Mr. Smith."

They came to Sheriff Bennett's door. Alexander jumped back on to his master's shoulder and Ponce de Leon Smith chuckled. "He is a great little fellow, Judge Bates. A comfort to me, sirs, you may be assured. My father admired Ponce de Leon, and a fearless man the explorer was, and I, in turn, admired Alexander the Great; therefore my pet's sterling name."

Alexander looked at Tobacco Jones and chattered rapidly. The lamplight streamed out of Bennett's open door to lay a yellow rectangle across the concrete floor. Bennett sat in the same position. Judge Bates was quick to note the spur rowel digging deeper into the desk.

"You have a visitor, Sheriff."

Bennett looked over Ponce de Leon Smith with a critical eye. "Blind beggar, eh?" Judge Bates noticed he used his usual lack of tact. "Heard you sawin' on that fiddle outside a while back."

"If I may correct you, sir, a violin — not a fiddle."

"They's fiddles to me," Bennett stated. "Well, what's on your mind, blind man? Time I'm gettin' t'home."

Ponce de Leon Smith told him that somebody had told him he had to have a peddler's license to operate in Singletree and that the license cost ten dollars. He was no peddler, he stated soundly; he was a dispenser of necessary merchandise. He sold pencils and horseshoe nails and gum and buttons. As he talked, he took a specimen of each bit of ware from his coat pocket.

"Still a peddler," Sheriff Bennett said stubbornly. "An' you need a license, or I'll float you out of town."

"But ten dollars, Sheriff — "

"Ten dollars," the sheriff said surlily.

Ponce de Leon bit his bottom lip in thought. Even Alexander, for once, was silent.

Tobacco chewed, scowling.

Judge Bates said, "That city ordinance, sir, is illegal." He cited a similar ordinance that had been protested and had been declared unconstitutional by the territorial court two years before. He showed that the judge had pointed out that community law was not as great as territorial or federal law and that such an ordinance violated the constitution of the United States.

"You come into this town, Judge, as

a person to sit on Judge Washburn's bench for a trial, if I might be so bold. You didn't come to run the burg." Bennett's voice was slightly threatening.

Tobacco stopped chewing. He knew one thing: you could advise Judge Bates — if you had the knowledge and brains to substantiate your statements — but you couldn't threaten him, even if he were wrong. The judge didn't scare worth a broken latigo strap.

"As county judge, I say this blind man can sell his wares freely on our streets, and without a license, Sheriff Bennett."

"I didn't mean to start trouble," Ponce de Leon Smith said.

"You are starting no new trouble, sir; you are only bringing to a climax the clash between me, the county judge, and this county upstart who, by circumstance, wears a law badge. You are free to sell your produce, and if he or his deputies bother you, I shall prosecute them to the fullest of my legal abilities. You may be sure of that, Mr. Smith."

Ponce de Leon Smith thanked the judge and hobbled out, cane rapping. Bennett said, "You talk big, Judge. Could you back those statements through the law?"

"Then you call me a liar?"

Bennett's hand rose. "No, no, do not misunderstand, Judge Bates!"

"Then your bald statements infer I do not know my high position, sir, and I do not know my law? Sir, I could arrest you for defacing county property. Look how your rowels gouge that desk."

"They ain't no law ag'in' a man puttin' his boots on his desk."

"Then again you call me a liar? When morning comes, come to my office, and I shall gladly show you the statute."

Bennett was thoroughly angry. His lean, sallow face was flushed, his lips trembled as he spoke. "I'll keep my boots here come hell or high water, law or no law! And nobody'll make me move them!"

The judge's boot kicked out and knocked the chair out from under Sheriff Bennett. The lawman hollered something, grabbed at the desk for support, and missed, to land sitting down on the concrete.

"Look me up," Judge Bates said, "and I'll show you that statute!"

6

WALT GALLATIN let the
trail-tired sorrels jog through
the dusk. The wind was down
and the scent of sage was in the still
thin air. Once a flock of sagehen flew
out of the sagebrush, wobbled as their
wings slowly lifted their heavy bodies.
Momentum and altitude gained, they
gathered speed and disappeared into
the encroaching darkness.

"You shouldn't worry about me,
Sarah. It seems foolish, you losing
your head, and rushing into town to
see if I was all right."

Sarah was worried, and her frown
showed it. She had seen Val Marcus
and Lew Basick ride toward Singletree,
she said, and with them had been Jim
Crow and the man called Blacky. "I
saw them through field-glasses when
they rode across the valley. I got afraid,

Walt, deadly afraid."

"I can take care of myself."

"But they laid a gun trap for you."

The young rancher pushed that aside with, "Oh, it wasn't that bad. I wish Judge Bates hadn't told you about it. I think he made it worse than it was. He should have kept his mouth closed. He told you that, and now you'll just worry."

Sarah Gallatin shook her head. "No. Judge Bates didn't want to scare me. He told me that so I would be prepared, if something did happen to you. He's afraid Marcus might kill you."

"He'll find me tough killin', Mammy."

They were silent then, with only the creak of the buggy and the plod of hoofs to break into their thoughts. Although Walt Gallatin had acted unconcerned about the matter, inside he was worried and serious. Judge Bates was right. Val Marcus intended to get rid of him by hook or crook, even if he stepped outside the pale of territorial law to get shut of him.

Until this afternoon, that fact had not been so real to him. But when Marcus and Basick and Blacky and Jim Crow had laid their trap — for one moment, then, the truth had been naked, and in that moment, he for the first time fully glimpsed his danger. Only the presence of Tobacco Jones in the Broken Latigo had saved him. Had Marcus recognized Tobacco Jones and known the lanky Cowtrail postmaster was Judge Bates' companion —

Walt Gallatin didn't finish that line of thought — it was too gruesome and terrible. Life to him was sweet: he had Sarah, and now they had little Mattie. He was young, terribly well, and he wanted to live for them and for himself. But had it not been for Judge Bates and Tobacco Jones, he'd've been dead now. And that thought still scared him.

"What do you say, Sarah?"

Mattie was sleeping, her head against her mother. Sarah tucked the blanket closer around their daughter's shoulders before answering. Behind the buggy,

Gallatin's saddle-horse trotted, tied to the end-gate.

"You make up your own mind, Daddy."

He knew that his wife was afraid — deadly afraid. But her fear was not for the Rocking R; it was for him. He himself had been orphaned at eleven, his mother and father and sister dying in a smallpox plague, and his uncle had reared him. He had put in four years at the university, where most of his time had been spent drinking hard liquor over the weekends and playing football and basketball and running the quarter-mile in track. His grades had just kept him eligible, and when he was a senior he had met Sarah, a freshman.

From then on, sprees were forgotten. He buckled down, made up deficiencies, and got his sheepskin. But his heart was with cattle, not with business. His uncle saw this and accordingly let him start a small cow outfit the spring before.

"Looks to me, Walt, as though this little girl has sure settled you down," Judge Hamilton Washburn had said.

Gallatin had admitted, rather forcefully that such was the case, and, with the baby on hand, he wanted to make a living the way he wanted, out on the range instead of in a store. But where could he find a good homestead to file on?

His uncle, rather uncertainly, told him about Broken Creek. He warned him, too, that Val Marcus had trailed Rocking R cows into the basin, and had run off a few nesters there. So the Gallatins had left Graybull and moved to Singletree. After the death of Joe Othon, Judge Washburn wished he had kept his mouth shut and had never mentioned Broken Creek.

For after Walt Gallatin had strung his barbwire fences around Broken Creek Springs, the trouble started.

Val Marcus had ridden up just about the time Gallatin had pounded the last staple firm into a diamond-willow fence post. "You're cuttin' my stock off from this water," he had reminded him.

Walt Gallatin had reminded him that he had legally filed on Broken Creek, and that, in addition to his original homestead of one hundred and sixty acres, Sarah used her homestead rights, also taking up a quarter section. In addition, they had also filed on desert claims, and that would give them another section, for a desert claim was three hundred and twenty acres.

"You control a section and a half of my grass, then?"

The grass, Gallatin had pointed out, did not belong to the Rocking R; the cow outfit had only been running on Government range. The Rocking R still had plenty of water in Wild Creek, Gumbo Springs, and other sources of water here on Singletree range.

"You still have plenty of water."

Marcus pointed out, rather baldly, that he intended to expand his herds, and would need the water. Gallatin told him to go to court for a settlement, if he thought he had one, and had climbed into his wagon and driven home. From the ridge he saw Marcus meet a rider and ride toward the Rocking R. He identified that rider as Lew Basick.

He did not realize it then, for his realization of the danger had not been as sharp as it later became. But Lew Basick had been on the ridge, hidden in the pines. And Basick had probably covered him with a rifle.

Later on, when he fully appreciated the trouble facing him, he realized that Val Marcus had ridden down, hoping to pick trouble with him. He had wanted him to draw his gun and then Basick, firing from concealment, would have killed him. And what could the court prove? Marcus would claim he had drawn first and he had killed him, not Basick. Basick would be Marcus' lying witness. And dead men couldn't talk in court.

The remembrance of his coming murder trial made him think of his talk with John Wimberley that afternoon. Wimberley was to plead his case in the coming trial; Wimberley, also, was clearing their titles to their homesteads. He had a clear title to his homestead on Broken Creek but, according to Wimberley, there was still much work to do to clear titles on Sarah's homestead and on the desert claims. He couldn't understand that, and he voiced his problem to his wife.

Sarah listened, nodding now and then, lips pursed in thought. Then she said, "Do you trust John Wimberley, Pappy?"

"I guess he's honest." He added, "As honest as the usual run of lawyer, anyway."

"Your uncle did not like him."

He had no answer to this. Judge Washburn was getting old and cranky, and he didn't like anybody any more, he figured. He decided to ask Judge Bates about John Wimberley. They were proving up titles to government grass, and there had been no previous owners . . . Why then this trouble to get deeds?

"How did Marcus and his men know I was upstairs with Wimberley? How did they know I'd left for town?"

Sarah had wondered about this, too. Maybe Marcus had had a spy concealed up on the rimrock, a rider who watched the Spur S through his glasses. This spy might have seen him leave and then ridden over to warn Marcus. Walt Gallatin admitted this plan seemed the most logical, and let it go at that.

They were in no hurry to get to the Spur S. Old Potter would have the two cows milked by now and would have the hogs fed, and ahead of them would be only the long fall evening. When they came to Wildcat Ridge, Sarah turned her head and said, "Walt, here comes a rider."

"Looks like Pete Rettiger," Walt said. "Now where is that deputy sheriff going?"

Sarah told him she had asked Judge

Lemanuel Bates to send out a deputy to guard the Spur S and its occupants. To this, Walt Gallatin said, "Woman, why did you do that? Old Potter and I can take care of our outfit. We don't need no protection from the law!"

"I think you do."

Walt Gallatin shrugged, wondered momentarily about women, then let the matter ride. Secretly, he was glad the deputy was coming to the Spur S — this was a load off his shoulders. But, being a man, he would not admit this, so he pretended he was angry.

"Where you heading for, Rettiger?"

Rettiger was a blocky man, short and wide of shoulder. His face was the color of an old saddle, beaten by storm and wind and sun. He told them that Sheriff Rube Bennett had ordered him to station himself at the Spur S.

"When you head out for the range, Walt, I'm supposed to ride with you, fella. Bennett says for you to feed me, an' he'll put in a claim for a refund with the commissioners the next time they meet."

"You're sure welcome, Pete," Sarah said.

Rettiger lifted his hand. "Thank you, Sary. Well, I'll lope ahead, Walt, an' wait for you. Ain't more'n a mile, be it?"

The deputy loped off, dust lifting idly behind his horse. Walt gigged the tired sorrels to a faster trot. He still couldn't understand clearly why Marcus wanted this range of his so badly. Marcus still had plenty of graze.

He decided, as he had reasoned so many times before, that, if he were allowed to settle on Rocking R grass, he would have driven a wedge into Marcus' outfit, for, with him there, other settlers would drift in. And that would mean Marcus' downfall as a cowman.

Other farmers, coming in via the new railroad, would see he had defied Val Marcus and, if one man had defied the cow king — and gotten away with it — why couldn't another man pull off the same trick? Therefore more settlers would come and more Rocking R range would be fenced.

No, Marcus could not let him stay, although legally he could settle on Broken Creek. Day by day the tension would grow up and become tighter and tighter until it would have to break.

He had tried to get his wife to take little Mattie and go back East for a visit for a few months. But Sarah, knowing full well he wanted her out of the way in case of danger, refused to go — her place, she reiterated, was with him. What kind of a wife would she be to run off when her husband needed her most?

She had made up her mind, he had seen, and he had abandoned that line of attack; then Joe Othon had been killed. He and Old Potter had lain along the fence, figuring somebody would try to cut it; they had lain there listening to the bull frogs croak in the rushes, listening to the wind in the cotton-woods and willows.

Old Potter had grasped his arm. "Rider out there, Walt."

They had lain silent, tense, listening. Below then had come the snip of wire-cutters; the fence beside them sagged, wire after wire falling slack. And they had gone ahead, crouched over their rifles, heading for the man with the wire-cutters. Joe Othon had seen them first.

He had run for his horse, his rifle marking the night with red flame. He had fired first, so they shot in self-defense. But the dark night made for uncertain shooting. Othon had his saddle when a bullet found him. It spilled him across his bronc's rump to the sod.

Old Potter had said, "He's dead, Walt. Dead."

Walt Gallatin was badly shaken. He got to one knee, not because he doubted Potter's words, but because he had to do something, for his nerves were screaming. He took Othon's limp wrist and felt for a pulse.

"Yes, he's plumb dead."

Old Potter's teeth had chattered. "This means wide-open range war, Walt. I wonder which one of us hit this hellion?"

Walt didn't know. They had both been firing. There in the darkness they had not found sights; they had just shot in Othon's general direction. His teeth wanted to chatter, too, but he held them gritted together.

"Yeah, range war . . ."

Things had broken fast, then. The next afternoon he was in jail on a murder charge filed by Val Marcus. The justice of peace had bound him over for trial in the superior court and his uncle had gone his bail. The county attorney, a just, square man, had said that Marcus had had enough evidence to warrant the issuing of a murder warrant.

Although he figured he would be cleared of the murder charge, he was still worried somewhat; trials had a way of back-firing, he knew. But with Judge Lemanuel Bates on the bench, there would be no dishonesty. Wimberley said he would come free. Marcus had no witnesses that they had shot Othon had he? Othon had ridden over to the fence alone. Both Old Potter and he would testify that Othon had shot first which he had. No, the court would clear them easily.

They came to the ridge and Broken Creek lay below them marked by cottonwoods and willows and rushes. The hoofs of their team sounded on the plank bridge and the iron rims of the buggy-wheels sang again in the dust.

"Gee, home sure looks good," Sarah said.

Walt Gallatin stopped the team in front of the barn. Deputy Pete Rettiger was squatting in front of the barn, cigarette in hand. "Thought you said Old Potter was home, Walt? They ain't nobody on the ranch."

Gallatin was unbuckling a tug. He

looked at him. "His horse was in the barn, Pete. That iron-gray gelding."

Rettiger said, "His bronc is still here, but Old Potter's gone. He must've pulled out on foot."

7

THEY came out of Sheriff Rube Bennett's office, and Marcus swung up and curbed his bronc around. "Now who is that reprobate?" he growled.

Lew Basick followed his boss' gaze. Marcus was looking at a thin man, evidently blind, who wore a comical coat and who had a monkey perched on his shoulder. The fellow stood in front of the Long Horn Restaurant, playing a violin. The noise was high-pitched and squeaky and rubbed against Marcus' nerves.

"Some blind beggar," Basick said.

Jim Crow said, "Don't worry about him, Marcus." He ran his forefinger gingerly across his right jaw. "The blind cain't see, and when you cain't see, you're not dangerous."

"My haid don't feel so good." The

man called Blacky rubbed his forehead and smiled.

Val Marcus took his gaze from the blind man and loped out of Singletree; Lew Basick at his right and Blacky at his left with Crow trailing behind. Evidently Jim Crow didn't like the dust for he pulled up even with Basick who regarded him with a wry smile.

"So you whipped Tobacco Jones, eh, Crow?"

Crow said, "Hang it, that ol' hellion can fight! Me, I figured he was easy; I know different now. He swung into action like a ostrich, all fists an' feet an' head. He butted me an' bit me an' even smashed in my toes. Next time I tangle with him, I'll use a club."

"Or a .45," Marcus said.

"That sheriff ain't no 'count to us," Basick finally said. "We shouldn't have elected him, Val. His badge has gone to his head."

"There's lots of vacant space for it," Marcus growled. "He'll help us indirectly — he's so dumb he'll never get wise to us. If a brainy man held that office, it would be dangerous for us, I'd say."

"This Jones gent ain't so ignorant," Basick said. "An' Judge Bates has plenty on the cue-ball, Marcus."

Marcus groaned, "Oh for God's sake, why bring them two up, Basick!"

Lew Basick looked at Jim Crow and winked. Marcus did not see the wink, and that was just as well. Secretly, Jim Crow and Blacky, tough men though they were, were a little afraid of Val Marcus, but not so Lew Basick. If Basick's albino eyes ever knew fear, they never showed it; they were always calm under their white eyebrows.

"You sure muffed that setup, Marcus."

Marcus looked hard and long at his range boss. He had never really understood Lew Basick and, secretly, he was a little afraid of the man. "Could you have done any better, Lew?"

"I couldn't have done worse."

Marcus took his gaze back to the trail

ahead. They were jogging along now, the run gone from their broncs; they were four riders in the twilight, the dust puffing lazily behind their horses, the jingle of bit and spur plain in the still air. Marcus said, "That Jones fellow fixed it for us."

"He fixed me, too," Jim Crow said dryly.

Blacky laughed at that, and Marcus smiled. But Lew Basick's pale eyes were without mirth, dull under white eyebrows. "Marcus, this thing is gettin' tight. Between the four of us, what is the next move?"

They were on a ridge, gray with sandstone rocks, some as big as a homesteader's shack, and below them a buckboard was going into Singletree. Marcus said, "That's our cook going into town for supplies, ain't it?"

Basick nodded, said, "I asked a question, friend."

Marcus kept watching the buckboard. "Sarah Gallatin's in town, too; her kid is with her. That leaves only Old Potter at the Spur S. Lew, we work the same old game. We pick on Gallatin, keep the country interested in that, and run the same old game on the side."

"A risky game, Val."

Marcus rolled a cigarette. "All games are risky, Lew; there's money in it. Fast, quick money, too. We'll make a stake here, the four of us, and then we'll sell out, lock, stock an' trigger — we'll leave the country. But when I hit the Argentine, I want plenty of dinero to buy that cow outfit I aim to run down on the pampas. An' I'll get that dinero out of this basin."

"But not out of cattle."

"Not out of cattle," Marcus confirmed.

Jim Crow asked, "Then why not quit botherin' young Gallatin? Some of us might get killed, boss."

Marcus stroked a match to life on his chap-wing. He had a small grin tugging his rough lips as he lit his cigarette. "Let one farmer get settled in here, Crow, and a hundred will come in inside of six months. We got a nice little game runnin' here; we got to keep these farmers out. And who knows — if we get through this deal okay — we might not head for South America. We might just stay here in Singletree grass."

Lew Basick shook his head. "You can't traffic with longriders, Val, and stay on the right side of the law. It ain't been done yet, and it won't be done."

Marcus shrugged.

They rode on, only now they did not hit for the Rocking R. They rode toward the Spur S. Finally Basick said, "Don't kill Ol' Potter, Val. If we do, the whole range will turn against us."

"Who said we aimed to kill him?"

Blacky said, "What's ahead, then? Burn down the Spur S?"

Marcus shook his head. "Neither, men. When we run Gallatin off, I want the Spur S buildings in good shape; why burn down property I can take possession of? We just aim to throw another scare into Walt Gallatin an' into the citizens in Singletree. Ol' Potter is just goin' to disappear."

They were on a lope again, four men strung out along the trail. And Val Marcus found the images of two men running through his memory with great vividness: one was a tall string-bean of a man, his face wrinkled and sear, his buckskin jacket draped around his slender shoulders. The other was a short, heavy-set man, wicked with his fists and shotgun — keen of brain and quick of eye. They had moved into this game and now they held cards, too.

They were the men to watch, the men to fear. Marcus was aware of this, terribly aware of it; this thought was something alive, something that bothered him, something that was always on the rim of his thoughts, something that gave him eternal worry. For a number of years, now, he had been kingpin on this range; he'd bossed it, and they had danced to his music. Then Walt Gallatin had come and Walt, seemingly, did not know how to dance or, if he did know a few steps, he was unwilling to show them off.

Walt had presented danger to him, a challenge he was quick to take. But each trap he had laid for the young rancher had, for some reason, sprung into his own face. Walt had been lucky, and Walt was smart.

Mostly lucky, Val Marcus figured. Although Walt was smart enough, too. He himself was no ignoramus. He would keep Singletree in turmoil, keeping the citizens on edge and uneasy, thus keeping them busy with their own troubles. And while they fretted and stewed in the trouble he had cooked up, he would continue to skim the broth off his other activity, the one that really paid him the money.

"Walt is shippin' in a well crew, I heard," Blacky grumbled.

"When they get casing down," Marcus declared, "it will suddenly blow up, men. Yes, sir, for some mysterious reason, that casing will explode, blocking

102

the hole and making them dig a new well."

"What does Wimberley say?" Basick wanted to know.

"Wimberley says he can hold up on them titles for months yet. Gallatin an' his missus don't know the titles are already in Wimberley's safe; they think they're still in Washington. Wimberley says that with him handling Gallatin's defense, Gallatin might be convicted."

"Not with Gallatin's friend, Judge Bates, on the bench." Jim Crow shook his long head.

Marcus reminded him that, from what he had heard, Judge Lemanuel Bates was honest on the bench, abiding by the evidence submitted. "Jim Crow, you and Blacky still aim to testify you rode with Joe Othon, the night they killed him?"

"For a thousand bucks," Jim Crow said, "I'd testify against my mother."

Basick scowled. "But that'll look funny, Marcus. At the preliminary trial, we never had a witness to the fight;

now suddenly we got two witnesses. Judge Bates will sure think that funny."

"He'll have to abide by the evidence, Wimberley says." Marcus flipped his cigarette away. "With Gallatin in the pen, we'll sure control this range. Any settler who aims to squat here will hear about what we done to Walt Gallatin, and he'll sure change his mind fast about becomin' a farmer on my grass."

They reached the creek below the Spur S. There they dismounted, tied their broncs in the high diamond-willows, and got their rifles out of saddle-boots. Marcus said, "Don't kill him unless you have to, savvy? Buffalo him, if you can; knock the old devil cold."

"Then what?" Blacky wanted to know.

Marcus said, "Leave that to me, friend. Now split up, all of you, and do as I outlined."

Evidently Old Potter was in the kitchen, cooking supper. Lew Basick sidled in beside the kitchen door and Marcus tossed a rock against the screen door. Basick heard Potter say, "What the heck was that? Sounded like little Mattie poundin' on the door, but she's in town."

They waited, listening to Old Potter and his pans.

Marcus pegged another rock out of the brush, this one rattling against the panel below the screen. The sound brought Old Potter out, an apron around his skinny middle, and the appearance of the old Spur S roustabout brought Lew Basick's rifle down. Potter's form went to the ground quickly.

"Reckon he recognized me?" Basick asked.

Marcus said, "He went out like a candle caught in a cyclone. He never had time to recognize you. Now gag the ol' devil an' tie his paws behind his back."

Soon they had Old Potter tied and gagged. Basick inspected him closely, feeling for a pulse, face a little pale as he knelt.

"He's alive," Marcus said. "They won't have *another* murder charge against you, Basick."

Basick said angrily, "Close your big mouth."

"He got a pulse?" Jim Crow asked.

Blacky was silent, watching.

Basick got to his feet. "He's alive," he confirmed. "Now, I'll get him up in my saddle, an' we'll ride like hell before he comes to an' recognizes us. Beaver Junction, eh, Marcus?"

"He'll *board* the train there," Marcus said.

They rode fast; it was only two or three miles to the railroad. They came over a hill and, true to Marcus' prediction, the evening freight train, heading west, was coming into Beaver Junction. The conductor slowed a little at this point, for here he picked up further orders. They pulled their broncs up close to the grade, dismounted, lugged Old Potter up on a small hummock, with Marcus holding his arms, Basick at the roustabout's feet.

"Still asleep," Basick said.

"Get him swinging," Marcus ordered.

The cars ran by and the train was gathering speed. They got old Potter swinging, and when a car came by with the door pushed back, they tossed him into the box-car. They saw him hit the floor, roll over; then the box-car had moved ahead, shutting off their vision.

"He'll wake up in that car, wonderin' where he is. He won't know how he got there. Well, we'll sure throw a scare into Walt Gallatin."

"Gallatin will think we killed him," Jim Crow said.

Basick kept watching the train. "Couldn't've been a bum in that car," he finally said. "If there had been, he'd looked out the door to see where Potter had come from. Potter'll never know what happened to him."

"He sure won't," Marcus said.

8

TOBACCO JONES was having breakfast in the hotel dining room when Maggie Shaw came in. Although he did not invite her, the newspaperwoman took a chair at his table, sitting beside him, not opposite him.

"You hear the news, Tobacco?"

Tobacco scowled, for she had not called him *Mr. Jones*. After all, they were practically strangers, and her tone was altogether too friendly.

"What news, Mrs. Shaw?"

Maggie ordered hot cakes, coffee, toast, bacon, eggs, potatoes, and a pork chop. Tobacco found himself wondering how her four husbands had ever managed to pay her grocery bill. Maybe that was one reason all four of them had taken to the brush, he decided.

The girl who waited table glanced at Tobacco, when Maggie did not see her, and smiled and shrugged her shoulder. Then she went into the kitchen, doors swinging behind her.

"Keep your eyes off her pretty back," Maggie advised. "You're old enough to be her great-great-grandfather."

Tobacco, irked, made no reply. Maggie Shaw remembered the news she was to impart. "Old Potter, the Spur S roustabout, has disappeared."

"He's *what*?"

Maggie elaborated. Her press had got into town ahead of schedule and she had had the city drayman haul it to her new office. Walt Gallatin had ridden in and reported to Sheriff Bennett that his *mozo* had disappeared. Bennett had ridden out, and he and Deputy Pete Rettiger had tried to find Old Potter.

"But they haven't found him yet. He isn't in town, and they've even ridden to the Rocking R, looking for him. Wonder where he went?"

"Maybe somebody's kilt him."

"Why?"

"Don't ask me why, or who." Tobacco held up his hand to silence her. "Sure, I know somethin' about writin' a news story, too. The five W's — who, what, when, where, why. Yeah, an' sometimes *how*." He got to his feet. "Wonder why Sheriff Bennett or Walt Gallatin didn't notify me or Judge Bates?"

Maggie told him that Walt had intended to notify them but she, thinking they were asleep, and tired, had talked him out of it. Tobacco Jones thanked her with wry humor. Just then Judge Bates, jowls blue-shaven, came into the dining room, and his partner told him about the disappearance of Old Potter.

"Maybe the old rascal has a girl friend somewhere, and is hiding out with her."

"Not with his face," Tobacco said sourly.

Tobacco went into the lobby, leaving the jurist talking with Maggie Shaw. He bought a plug of Horseshoe from the clerk, bit off a chew, and then glanced up to see Ponce de Leon Smith coming down the stairs, Alexander on his right shoulder, his violin case hanging from a sling on his other shoulder. Ponce de Leon was jabbing with his cane at the steps.

The Cowtrail postmaster thought it odd that a man, seemingly a bum, could make enough money to live in the hotel, and then decided may be he should take up soliciting on the streets. Ponce de Leon reached the bottom step; he stood, cane moving back and forth, reaching for the next step.

"One more, Mr. Smith, and you are on the floor, sir."

The dark glasses lifted toward the postmaster. The thin lips said, "Thank you, Mr. Jones." The man hobbled toward the dining room, cane rapping in front of him, and as they went through the big doorway, Alexander blew a kiss back at Tobacco Jones.

"Cute little devil," the clerk volunteered.

Tobacco went out into the fall sunshine. The wind was chilly, despite the sun, and he looked at the encircling mountains, figuring that any day now the first snow of the year would hit them. The drayman was carrying some rolls of paper into Maggie Shaw's office and he, out of curiosity, went that way.

"Give me a boost with this, bud?"

Tobacco helped him. The place was a mess. Type in one box, the press in the middle of the floor. Tobacco looked at the press and pushed its handle. It moved hard. Well, Maggie was a lot of woman; she could move it back and forth. She had the weight and brawn.

Maggie Shaw came in. She beamed a smile at Tobacco and said, "Mr. Jones, will you help us move this press? It is just too heavy for me and the drayman."

Tobacco assured her, too hurriedly, that he was no hand at lifting; he had hurt his back, he claimed, in the war.

"The War of 1812?"

"No, the Revolutionary War."

"Let's not get too complicated," Maggie said.

They got hold of the press, the drayman on one corner, Maggie and Tobacco on the other. She wanted it, she said, in the exact center of the floor, and Tobacco, not too well pleased with the affair, reminded her that, if it was in the center, it would be *exact*. At that, Maggie glanced sharply at him, seemingly satisfied.

"I'd like you for a reporter, Tobacco."

"Not me, madam."

They got the press off the floor, and Maggie suddenly let her end down. The beam landed across Tobacco's instep, bringing a yowl of pain from him. Quickly Maggie grabbed and lifted the weight.

"Hurt your foot, Tobacco?"

Tobacco said sarcastically, "Oh, no, it didn't hurt a bit." He looked at her big-knuckled hands grasping the bed of the press. "Now how come your hand managed to slip? And it seems odd that this hit me across the instep just like that satchel of type hit you yesterday when I bounced into you."

"Just a coincidence," Maggie assured him. "My first edition will be out tomorrow, I guess. The headlines, of course, will be about old Potter."

The drayman, between pants, declared that old Potter might've drunk so much he had changed into liquid, thereby running down a crack in the gumbo and disappearing. Tobacco judged the man had no great admiration for the old roustabout, both as a character and as a drinking man.

Tobacco went outside and crossed the street and met the judge in the hotel's lobby, where His Honor had planted his heavy carcass deep into a leather-backed easy chair, where he pondered on the world as he picked his teeth. Maggie Shaw had also informed the jurist about old Potter's disappearance.

"What d'you figure happened to him, Bates?"

The jurist removed his toothpick and

scowled. "I am sure I don't know, friend. You don't suppose they have killed him?" Then he answered his own question. "No, that isn't logical. Old Potter isn't dangerous to Val Marcus. He's just a doddering old-timer and no more."

Tobacco asked if Potter had headed over toward the Reservation. "There's some nice-lookin' squaws over there, Bates."

"Do you speak from experience?"

Tobacco said, "Ah, can that talk, Judge. You don't reckon he got scared and pulled stakes, do you?"

"He might have."

Tobacco said, "Let's ride out to Walt's an' look around."

"That's a long ways," the judge said slowly. "Me, I don't feel like riding in this wind. I judge that Sheriff Bennett will head into town soon. Let's go to my office and see if the janitor has a good warm fire."

"You're gettin' old," Tobacco grumbled.

They went down the street, with Tobacco Jones limping a little, and the jurist, upon inquiring what made the sudden impediment in his partner's walk, got the hot anwer that Maggie Shaw, deliberately and purposefully, had dropped a corner of the press on his instep.

"Sue her," the judge advised smilingly.

Tobacco had no answer to this. The janitor, as usual, had no fire going in the legal chambers; while Tobacco started one, the judge had his after-breakfast drink. Tobacco, once the old newspapers got burning, put some dry pine knots in the pot-bellied heater.

Down by the Long Horn Café, Ponce de Leon Smith had his violin going, the squeak of it sounding dismal and cold. Tobacco, watching out the window, asked, "And how does that blind gent stand his own music?"

"Maybe he's deaf, too."

"I can't savy him, Bates. Surely they must be better towns than this cow-dog burg to bum in. Places where there are more people and more dinero."

"Every man," the jurist said, "is his own master."

Tobacco Jones, not being in a philosophical mood, did not pursue the problem any further. He moved his skinny carcass close to the heater and absorbed some of its warmth. The sounds of Ponce de Leon's violin seeped through the closed windows, and he tried to make out the tune the blind man was supposedly playing.

"Sounds like *La Paloma*, Bates."

"Sounds like murder to me."

Tobacco watched young Walt Gallatin ride into view. Walt tied his horse to the hitchrack in front of the courthouse and came inside. His square, blocky face showed his worry.

"I sure cain't figure out what happened to old Potter, men. His clothes are still at home, and his supper, still cooking, was on the stove. His bronc was in the barn, too. That means he never rode out, and if he hiked out, why didn't he take his clothes?"

"Something has happened to him," the judge said.

Walt was silent. Then, "I thought a lot of the old man, gents. If he's dead — killed — Marcus will pay and pay plenty."

Judge Bates told him, rather crisply, to forget such talk. What evidence, if any, had he that pointed toward Marcus' meddling into this Potter's affair? None, Walt replied. But he had his suspicions, didn't he?

"But suspicions, Walter Gallatin, do not hold up in a court of law. What a court needs is direct evidence — the evidence of competent witnesses. You are making guesses, basing sentences upon mere premises, sir."

"Marcus is behind this, I tell you."

The judge questioned him further. No, he had not found tracks leading away from the Spur S. Down by the creek, it looked as if horses had waded in the water, but he had some range horses around there, and maybe they had left the tracks, not saddle horses and riders. Yes, he'd looked for Potter along the brush, but had found no trace of him.

"This has got Sarah scared to the bone, men. She thinks sure something will happen to me, now; she's pale around the gills." Walt Gallatin smiled.

"You look kind pale yourself," Tobacco stated.

"I'm not running, though." Gallatin pulled his gun-belt around, moving his weapon closer to the front. "I feel like gettin' Val Marcus alone — if it's possible — and getting him into a fight with me. But it's hard to get the scissorbill alone, men — he always packs a few guards with him."

Judge Bates reminded him he was out on bond, for murder. And if Gallatin persisted in such talk he, as county judge, would possibly be forced to retract the rancher's bail, putting him back in the calaboose again. "A threat, sir, is a dangerous thing. A threat is but a forerunner of violence,

Walt. To stop violence, you must go to the core of the matter, destroying the elements that lead to violence. I want to hear no more such talk from you."

"Am I going to sit still, Your Honor, and let myself get pushed around? Is that what you want me to do?"

"I want you to keep a clear head, sir."

Gallatin lost his anger, thought this over, and admitted the judge was right. He intended, he said, to search more thoroughly along the creek, for old Potter might have fallen in and drowned. Lately the old rider had taken to hitting the bottle pretty hard, and Sarah had made a rule he could not keep a bottle on the premises. So old Potter had cached his hard liquor down along the creek.

Walt Gallatin rode to the store, came out with a fifty-pound sack of flour, tied this behind his saddle, and rode out of town, heading for the Spur S. Thirty minutes later, Sheriff Bennett rode in, left his bronc at the tie-rack, and stomped into the hall, cursing the cold wind.

"Any luck, Bennett?"

"Nary a bit, Bates." Bennett sank disgustedly in his swivel chair. The county clerk had shoved his mail on his desk, and the sheriff sorted it sourly, looking at the *man-wanted* placards. "Sure a lot of gents on the dodge, ain't they, though?" He looked closely at one picture. "Man, I've seen this gent lately, I have. I know I have, men." He looked up hard at Judge Bates.

"He isn't me," the judge assured him.

Bennett seemed to hold no ire against the jurist. He leaned back in his chair, thumbs hooked in his vest. "Now where t'hades has ol' man Potter went? This has got me, men. Maybe he did go over the reservation to see the squaws, at that. But I got a wire off to the agent over there; he h'ain't seen whisker or shoe of him."

"That reservation is big, though,"

Tobacco Jones said.

Judge Bates nodded.

Bennett said, "I hate to say this, but I figure he might be dead. He might've got drunk an' felled in the crick. Sary made him keep his bottle out in the brush. If'n he did get drowned, could I raise hob with Sary for that, Judge?"

"Use your head," the judge murmured.

9

BRACED against the cold fall wind, the partners went toward the depot, still unpainted and new. Tobacco Jones grunted sarcastically, "We runnin' off, Bates? We catchin' a train out?"

"You sound cold, friend."

Tobacco admitted, rather sourly, he was far from dying of heat. The wind, cold from the snow in the high mountains, bit through their sheepskin coats. Winter would be here soon, and the postmaster found himself dreading the oncoming cold. "Wish that court trial would come an' get itself over with, Bates, an' then we could go back home."

"Just as cold in Cowtrail, friend."

"Sure, but I can stay close to my post office heater all day, not traipse up an' down a windswept country." He swiveled his head around and regarded his partner. "Why for are we headin' for the depot?"

"You'll see."

The depot was warm, with lignite making the heater red. They warmed themselves in the waiting room, listening to the click of the telegrapher's key. The operator was a skinny, short man with a huge bald head, and, strapped over his glistening dome was his ear-phone. He looked up at them with a blank face, did not acknowledge their presence, and then glanced away, listening in a vague sort of way to his key.

The judge, his hands finally warmed, moved toward the window. Finally the operator asked, "Something, men?"

The jurist introduced himself and his partner. He asked if Sheriff Rube Bennett had sent out wires to various surrounding lawmen, inquiring if they had seen anything of old Potter. The agent said he could not answer this, for what business he did with the sheriff was, of course, confidential.

"But I am the county judge, sir."

"The *acting* county judge," the agent corrected. He reminded the jurist again that he was bound by the law to keep any messages sent out by the sheriff secret. Tobacco growled something, his voice low and displeased, and Judge Bates hurriedly assured him the agent was correct. At this, the agent smiled a little, but it was a rather sour attempt.

Thereupon the judge took paper and pencil and Tobacco watching over his shoulder, saw him write:

'Singletree County Judge Lem Bates asks the co-operation of local officers in locating the whereabouts of one Potter, first name James, who disappeared on evening Sept. 24 from ranch of local resident. Foul play feared. Description follows.'

The judge described the old man, then listed the officers who were to receive the message. This done, he told the agent to submit his bill to the county, and he would see that the next meeting of the commissioners refunded him the expenses. The agent went to work immediately, tapping out the message to other key-men up and down the line.

The partners went back into the raw wind. Tobacco asked, "Where to now, Bates?" and the jurist replied, "Out to the Rocking R, I'd say."

"We won't be welcome out there."

They went to the livery, where the jurist tied his jug on behind his saddle. They rode out into the wind again, riding directly into it, heads pulled low into sheepskin collars, with Tobacco mumbling and grumbling. The judge, who knew the folly of cursing the weather, was silent and let his thoughts have their way with him.

They were half way to the Rocking R when they met Maggie Shaw. She rode a big gray gelding, evidently a work-horse, and, for some reason, she reminded the judge of Don Quixote, for the horse had to bear an enormous weight. She caught his sly grin and glared at him.

"What're you grinning about, Judge Bates?"

"Grinning, madam? Surely you must be mistaken. Perhaps the cold weather has put a look on my face you mistake for a grin."

"I'd sure hate to see your mug get frozen that way," she said cattily. "Now where are you gents heading for?"

They told her they were riding for the Rocking R. She said she had just come from that ranch, after having quite a verbal battle with Val Marcus. "I questioned him rather closely about the disappearance of old Potter. He grew rather incensed, too, and reminded me the sheriff had just questioned him, and if I wanted to know anything, why didn't I go to the sheriff."

"He has his rights," the judge murmured.

"Yes, and so has my newspaper.

Gentlemen, I am going to write a hot editorial against Mr. Marcus; I do not like his ways or his personality. I have the lead already running through my mind."

"He won't like it," Tobacco pointed out.

"The cornerstone of our liberty, Mr. Jones, is laid on the premise that our press is free. Many a libel case I have fought out in court — and won, too. I believe I shall turn back and ride with you gentlemen."

"We're old enough to take care of ourselves," the judge reminded her. He definitely did not want the woman along. The way he looked at it, he and Tobacco had enough trouble, as it were, without having this gad-about hook up with them. If she persisted in coming, he would definitely tell her she couldn't come.

"I'd like to hear what you say to Mr. Marcus."

"We might not even ride there," the judge said. "We might just mosey around the range, looking for a trace of old Potter."

Instantly the jurist knew that Maggie Shaw did not believe him. For one thing, as she deliberately pointed out, the weather was too cold to 'mosey around,' and, in her mind, she was convinced old Potter was dead.

"Marcus and his gang have killed the old devil, Mr. Bates. They want to scare Mr. and Mrs. Gallatin out of this country. With Old Potter disappearing like this, into thin air — well, the Gallatins are going to get afraid, I swear."

"Don't swear out loud," Tobacco Jones grunted.

The partners rode on, leaving Maggie Shaw sitting her horse and watching them. Once Judge Bates, who kept glancing back, saw her ride toward them. Then she checked her bony plough-horse and turned him back toward Singletree. Tobacco bit off a chew and allowed she was just a nuisance.

"Aren't all women a nuisance, Jones?"

"Some aren't, Bates. They're good cooks."

If the jurist had an answer for this, he did not state it. He did not intend to ride into the Rocking R. He wanted to leave his bronc in the brush and scout the out-buildings for, by some chance, perhaps Old Potter was being held here. But that, reason told him, was hardly logical.

"Field glasses up yonder on the mountain." Tobacco Jones spoke suddenly. "I seen the flash of them, Bates."

"Ride on like you never noticed it, Tobacco. Then when we get hidden in yonder grove of willows, we'll do a little scouting. You got your field glasses on your saddle, haven't you?"

"Never ride without them, Bates." Tobacco added a dig. "You carry your jug, I carry my glasses."

They jogged on, seemingly without a worry, and, when they reached the willows, they drew rein, looking upward at the mountain and its black spruce and pine and rocks. The postmaster's mitten pointed out the exact spot of the flash.

"And I knowed it was the flash of the sun on glass, Bates. What else could it be, but that?"

The judge reminded him that somebody might have dropped a bottle up on the side of the mountain.

"And what fool would drink up on that danged peak? Bates, sometimes I think you're addled."

Smiling, the judge assured him he himself had drunk on the sides of mountains, some steeper than the one they were looking at. When a man got thirsty, the jurist said, he'd drink anywhere, even sitting on top of an elephant.

"That bottle," Tobacco said, "is ridin' away."

Sure enough, a rider was leaving the timber, heading over the mountain. The judge grabbed the field glasses and hurriedly adjusted them but, by that time, the man had disappeared, the mountain behind him shutting him out of view. The jurist scowled, lowered the glasses. "That wasn't Maggie following us, was it?"

Tobacco shook his head. "Not big enough for that female moose, Bates."

Judge Bates chuckled, the sound deep in his thick chest. "Maggie's got her eyes on you, Tobacco. I watched her a while back — she looked at you when you weren't looking, and she smiled so soft and pretty. Funny, fellow, how these big fat women always fall for you. Is it because you're so thin, and opposites attract?"

"You figure that out, Bates." Tobacco's frown changed into anger. "Bates, we ride out in this cold, lookin' for some clue to ol' Potter. We got a young friend in trouble — serious trouble — we got to help him. Yet you set here like a full raccoon and grin and joke about a homely woman!"

"Hold your broncs, friend!"

They rode up the creek, bronc

laboring against the incline. They reached the divide, the wind howling worse than ever, and they saw the rider below them, going toward Singletree.

The glasses showed Judge Bates that Tobacco had been right: The rider was not Maggie Shaw. The distance was too far for actual identification. The judge focused the glasses to their sharpest point and watched the back of the rider disappear.

For some reason, something was vaguely familiar about the rider — the set of his shoulders, his build. But the thing was wavering, nebulous; the parts would not fit, for the whole of the pattern shifted too rapidly. Disgusted, he returned the glasses to his partner.

"Don't know, Tobacco."

"Rider almost out of sight, Bates," grumbled Tobacco, "an' you hand me these things, figurin' I can identeefy him."

Tobacco looked, jaw steady, chew bulging in his cheek. Finally he lowered the glasses and his jaw took up its normal rhythm. He rubbed his mitten across his forehead, then winced a little. "Forehead's still sore where that Jim Crow fella busted me, Bates."

"Any luck?"

Tobacco shook his head. "No, I should know him — he's danged familiar — but I can't place him, right now. Looks to me he's headin' for Singletree, ain't he?"

"Looks that way."

The rider went out of sight against the wind and the distance. The pair rode toward the Rocking R, both trying to place the rider, both having no luck. They were riding along the creek when they came upon another horseman. This man was not watching them, though; he had merely cut across the creek, and they came upon him unawares. The judge thought he read surprise in the square, unshaven face, but it was hard to tell, for the man's red whiskers were rather long.

"Howdy," the judge said.

The man grunted, "Hello, gents,"

and reined in, watching them through bloodshot eyes. The judge figured he was a real tough customer, judging from his clothes, none of which were any too clean, and from the unshaven face with the bloodshot eyes and the thick lips marked with dried tobacco juice.

"Ride for the Rocking R?" the jurist asked.

"See any Rocking R brand on my hoss?"

The man's tone was plainly unfriendly. Judge Bates felt anger arise, then decided against it. Evidently the stranger saw this, too, for his tone, for some reason, became a little friendlier.

"Jes' ridin' acrost country, men. Had a job punchin' dogies down aroun' Cowtrail for a coupla friends of mine, Judge Lem Bates an' Tobacco Jones. Ever hear of them two?"

The judge glanced at Tobacco Jones. The post-master stopped chewing a moment, and then, catching the judge's cue, resumed his pulverization of his tobacco. The judge assured the man he had never heard of Judge Bates and Tobacco Jones.

"Nice men to work for," the man said. "Well, have to mosey along, gents. I'm skippin' Singletree. Boy back yonder told me there was no work around here. Reckon I'll drift up to Graybull. Well, so long."

The man loped off, leaving the partners sitting their broncs. The brush rose and hid him. Only then did Judge Bates say, "Somebody's loco, friend, and it isn't we two. That fellow worked for us, he says, and yet he didn't know us. But his memory must be as bad as mine, at that, because I sure don't remember him on our payroll, do you?"

"He never worked for us, Bates."

"Then why say he did?"

"He wanted to impress us with the fact he was riding across the country. He tried so hard that he brought in the fact he had worked around Cowtrail. Now we know that ain't true." The jurist was going down from his bronc. "Give me those glasses again!"

They left their bronc hidden and walked up the side of a steep hill, the wind behind their backs. They were both puffing when they reached the altitude they wanted. Here in the sandstones they halted, but they could not see the rider below. Tobacco spat and admitted the man could not ride out of sight in such a short time.

"But we can't see him, Jones."

"Over there, Bates."

For some reason, the rider has switched directions; now he was riding toward the Rocking R, perhaps three miles away. They watched the man ride into the yard of the Marcus Ranch and put his bronc in the barn. Judge Bates lowered the glasses, scowling a little.

"Now what is this all about, Jones?"

10

WHEN Walt Gallatin and his wife and baby reached town, the young rancher stopped his team in front of the Broken Latigo Saloon. He helped Sarah down, and she went into the Mercantile with the baby while her husband tied the team to the tie-rack. Then Gallatin went upstairs to see John Wimberley.

He nodded at Smokey, the bartender, had a short drink, then climbed the stairs, remembering that, but a few hours before, death had faced him on these same stairs — death had looked at him from the guns of Marcus and Basick and Blacky. This thought was not pleasant. It was like the hall down which he walked — cold and drafty.

"Come in," Wimberley's voice said.

The lawyer, dressed in a pin-stripe blue suit, sat at his desk, papers scattered before him. The stove cast out its warmth, and Walt Gallatin, hands behind his back, absorbed the warmth.

"This kind of makes me wish I had had brains enough to study law in school, and not look only at a football and the bottom of a bottle held up against the moon."

Wimberley leaned back, drumming long, bony fingers on the desk. He asked if they had found old Potter yet and then, on finding they had found no trace of the old man, he voiced amazement, wondering what had happened. Gallatin had no answer to this, for he had no idea what had happened to the roustabout, either.

"I certainly do not understand it, Walt."

Gallatin reminded him that it wasn't old Potter's custom to disappear suddenly. The old man had been very conscientious about this, for he knew there was trouble abroad, and he always let them know where he was going, if only out to tighten a barb-wire in the horse pasture. He switched the subject over to the deeds that he and his wife had coming.

Wimberley shook his long, hangdog face thoughtfully. No, the deeds had not arrived; they were evidently being held up in Washington, D.C. Yes, he had sent a letter — a long letter — to the territorial capital, requesting some action on these deeds, but he had not received a reply as yet.

"The territorial governor might be able to push these through faster, sir. Although, as you know, there is no hurry."

Gallatin frowned and reminded him that, if a deed didn't go through in a year, another party could try to homestead on a piece of property. And he didn't want to lose his land to the Rocking R and Val Marcus.

"You have months yet."

"Only three months, sir."

Wimberley's face showed surprise. "I'll try to hurry it faster, Walt. I'll write to Washington and to our representative there. The governor might get things rolling." He added, "I know him personally."

Gallatin found himself thinking that Wimberley, judging from past conversations, evidently knew a lot of important men. He said that perhaps Judge Bates could help get the deeds through sooner. Wimberley scowled at this, and he got the impression the lawyer did not want Judge Bates' opinion, yet Wimberley said that this might be a good idea.

"Although, Walt, Bates can do nothing I cannot do."

They talked over the coming trial, then, their business completed, Gallatin went down the stairs, glad indeed that Val Marcus and Lew Basick and Blacky did not have a surprise party for him this time. Only Judge Bates and Tobacco Jones were in the saloon.

"Where's Smokey, Judge?"

"Out behind, filling my jug from a barrel. Have a drink, Walt?"

Gallatin agreed that a drink would feel good, for the wind was chilly outside, and the judge, leaning his fat person across the wide corner, with much grunting and groaning procured Smokey's private bottle, hidden under the bar. He speared two glasses off the rack and filled each to the brim.

Gallatin glanced at Tobacco Jones, who said, "Never touch the hog-wash," and the rancher raised his glass, drinking his whisky clean. By that time, Judge Lem Bates had killed his drink, and they went down to base-rock and talked business. Old Potter was still among the missing. And the deeds had not come through yet. And they had only three months left to procure them.

"We were just down the depot," Tobacco Jones said. "Your well-drillin' outfit is in on siding on a flat car an' the crew is comin' in on the next passenger train, I guess. Where at do you aim to put down this casin'?"

Only one place to put it down,

Gallatin said, and that was on the north corner of the horse pasture, for this was the highest piece of land, and water would drain in any direction from that point.

"Besides, I got my deed for that piece of land. If I put it on any of the other pieces, and I lost them by not getting my deed within the required time, I'd lose an expensive well, too."

Sheriff Bennett came in, lean and lanky as ever, and started questioning Gallatin about Old Potter. Smokey came back and said, "Three dollars, Judge," and the jurist paid him and he and Tobacco left, the judge carrying his jug under one arm. Sarah Gallatin was coming out of the Mercantile, arms filled with bundles, and they helped her load them in the buggy. This done, Judge Bates chucked Mattie under the chin, and asked Sarah if he could give her daughter a drink, joking all the while. Sarah grimaced and said no.

"But we want you two out for supper some night soon, Judge. We'll set the date later on, eh?"

The partners agreed, saying the date should be soon. Then they resumed their way toward the courthouse. Tobacco grinned and declared, to his way of thinking, that Sarah Gallatin was against drink, for hadn't she made Old Potter keep his bottle off the Spur S Ranch proper?

"And why shouldn't she, sir? Could Old Potter control his desire for hard drink? No, he was helpless — one drink led to another — they all led to a drunken stupor. I do not blame the young woman one bit, sir."

They walked down the cold corridor of the courthouse, the judge rumbling dire things directed toward stingy county commissioners who would not even allot a big enough sum to keep the courthouse warm. Sheriff Bennett's office, as usual, was open, the door swung in, and this drew further rumblings from the jurist. Bennett was a fool, an idiot — why didn't he shut his door? Anybody could sneak in and steal a confidential paper from the desk.

"Bet he don't even look at half the mail he gets," Tobacco volunteered. "A bank robber could josh with him on the street, and Bennett would never recognize him."

Once in the judge's office, they hung their sheepskins on the coat rack, and the jurist, with great gusto, stirred the coals in the stove, noisily slapping the coal hod against the steel as he emptied the hod's contents into the stove. Evidently he gave the stove the right medicine for it roared into life and heat sprang out from its thick sides.

Tobacco, warming his hands, remembered the rider who had seen them through field glasses, and he wished again, trying hard to identify the rider, that he could get one of those quick flashes in his mind telling him what he wanted to know. But this did not come, a fact that greatly irked him.

Judge Bates, glasses on now, was studying his mail. He opened one letter, and the shaven, clean face of a man of about twenty-five, sleek and well-groomed, looked at him. Tobacco moved closer.

"You get them placards, too, Bates? Thought only the sheriff of the county got them pictures of wanted men."

The judge said these were also sent to the judge and county attorney. He studied the sleek, almost feminine face, then tossed the placard aside. Tobacco picked it up and studied it, too.

"Funny, that gent looks soft an' nice, don't he? Yet he's wanted for first-degree murder down in Colorado. He don't look like he'd harm a mouse."

"Never tell by looking at a face, Tobacco."

Tobacco asked if the judge had other circulars. The judge pulled open a bottom drawer of the desk, and there Judge Hamilton Washburn had filed the photos according to alphabetical order of names.

"But he never even looked into these after filin' them, Bates. He's so near

146

sighted he couldn't see a billy goat hit him in the belly."

The judge, reading a letter, grunted something. Tobacco squatted on the floor, sitting cross-legged like a Sioux buck, his back to the stove, and looking at the placards in the file.

Slowly the judge's leonine head dropped to rest on his chest, and soon he was breathing heavily. This breathing was changing into snoring when Tobacco Jones, plainly excited, tugged on his partner's coat, finally awakening the jurist.

"Can't you let a man sleep, Tobacco?"

"Look, Bates!"

The postmaster shoved a placard in front of his partner's nose. Grumbling, Judge Bates took it, moving it out further so he could see it better. The man was young, in his twenties, and his face was blocky. There was a hard, determined look around his eyes and lips.

"What about him?"

"Put whiskers on him, Bates. Imagine

he had whiskers."

Judge Bates said, "Oh, oh," and read, "Mack Byson, bank robber, killer, wanted . . . " He looked at his partner. "That's the gent we met out in the hills, Tobacco; the guy that swung around and then rode into the Rocking R."

Tobacco said, "I'd say it was him, Bates." He got to his feet, putting the placards back in the drawer, still holding the picture of Mack Byson. He studied the portrait again. "Of course, we might be mistook, Bates. But me, I figure if we could pull a sharp razor across that gent's mug, he'd look like this Byson gent when we got done."

Again, Judge Bates studied the portrait. Then he shook his head slowly, mumbling, "We might be wrong, Jones. I've seen a number of cowboys that could almost fill this bill."

"But not as good as that gent can," the postmaster maintained.

Judge Bates leaned back, fingers laced across his big belly. "Marcus might be running something shady, too, Jones. The best thing we can do is sit back, watch and listen, and keep our mouths shut."

"Let's head out to the Rockin' R, Bates, an' bring this son in, eh?"

Judge Bates did not open his eyes. But a smile flicked across his thick lips. "Friend, outside the weather is bad; we just came from the Rocking R. This will keep. Never rush into anything . . . unless you know for dead certain you are right. I wonder just where John Wimberley stands in this picture?"

"That Byson gent might pull out of the Rockin' R, Bates."

"And that might not even have been Mack Byson."

Tobacco walked to the window. Outside, snow was falling a little, not steadily, just an occasional flake, scurrying past as the hard wind drove it. The thin, uncertain wail of a violin came through the pane, the wind hurrying it along with the snowflakes.

He watched Ponce de Leon Smith

leave the Mercantile, Alexander running on his leash beside him. Again the terrible pitch of the violin sounded and again the postmaster mentally agreed with himself that this man was the worst violinist he had ever heard. Surely the man must be deaf, or totally without an ear for music!

The violinist went into the Broken Latigo Saloon. Suddenly memory washed across Tobacco Jones, and he was rudely shaking Judge Lem Bates out of a sound sleep. Judge Bates, roughly awakened, glared in righteous anger at his partner.

"I say, Tobacco, let me nap!"

"Bates, listen. I was just watchin' Ponce de Leon Smith, an' now I remember. Mind that strange rider out yonder — the one thet watched us with field glasses? Mind how we both almost recognized him?"

"Yeah."

"That rider," Tobacco said, "was Ponce de Leon Smith."

Judge Bates gave this a moment's

thought. Then, "Yes, the rider did resemble him, somewhat. But surely you are not serious? For how could a blind man ride out there on that rough peak? And what good would it do him? What could he see?"

"Sure appeared like him, Bates."

11

CAREFULLY John Wimberley locked the two windows, banked the lignite heater, and went out into the cold, drafty hall, locking his door behind him and testing the lock to make sure it had caught. He rubbed his long, bony hands together, the knuckles blue with cold, and he put on his mittens and went down into the Broken Latigo Saloon, walking slowly down the creaking steps.

"Rum, Smokey, with a dash of water."

While Smokey mixed the drink, John Wimberley looked around the saloon's interior, marking the card game in the corner, nodding at an acquaintance sitting on a pool table. He sipped his drink, thinking of the cold ride he had ahead, and not relishing a foot of the distance he had to cover.

"An early winter, Smokey?"

"I prophesy one, Mr. Wimberley. I've had that hitch in my leg for almost a week now, and that means cold weather is coming."

John Wimberley nodded, smiling. While Smokey explained the mysteries of his leg — the left one — Wimberley nodded occasionally, but his thoughts were miles away. He admitted that he had heard of cases where people could predict weather changes by the behavior of their rheumatism and aches and pains. He finished his rum and water, bought a bottle of Scotch — which he put in his sheepskin pocket — and went outside, where the snow was a little thicker now. The wind had died down, for evening was close at hand, and that, he decided, helped some. For he hated the wind.

He met Sarah Gallatin, coming out of the Brown residence, and he lifted his hat, a smile breaking his gaunt features. Walt was down looking at his well-digging outfit, for it was on a flat-car down on siding, and when he got done there they would go home. Little Mattie started to bawl.

Wimberley decided he, too, would like to look over the well-digging equipment. Not that he was interested in it, but after all Gallatin was his client, and he should show some interest in him and his doings.

Walt Gallatin was up on the flat-car, looking over the equipment, when John Wimberley's long form came out of the dusk. Behind them the kerosene lamps of the town winked and blinked, showing the slanting, falling snow. A dog howled in cold misery, and beyond the edge of the town a coyote answered in cold reply.

"Quite an outfit." Gallatin came off the flat-car to stand beside the barrister. "Reckon there must be at least five men in the crew, huh, judging from the size of that bit. They even had the casing I need. Looks to me like they got some fourteen-inch casing, I'd guess."

Wimberley admitted that a big casing like that could carry lots of water. Gallatin was very enthusiastic. "Get water on my land, John, and it will bloom, I tell you. That soil is good, with darned little alkali in it, and when it gets plenty of good water, it sure will sprout crops. Then the Rocking R can never hold its range; farmers will come in by the hundreds, I maintain. Once the farmers see what irrigation will do they'll flock in, John."

Wimberley wondered about the water-table. On one particular range he had graced by his presence — he did not give the name of the town — deep wells had lowered the water-table so severely the wells had gone dry. The wells had been dug deeper and then had lowered again as the water had been pumped out. That particular community, of course, had had some dry years, with no rain in the summer and very little snow in the winter; but hadn't they had five dry years around Singletree? Or so he had heard, anyway.

Walt Gallatin assured him that the state geologist guaranteed an unlimited amount of water in the local water-table, saying that it could never be pumped dry, for it found its source in the mountains. Wimberley had no answer to this, but wanted to know when they would start digging a well. Gallatin said, "As soon as possible, John. I wish we had the deeds to those other pieces of land. I'd like to start on that east eighty, but I reckon I'll put the first well down in my horse pasture."

"Those deeds will come through soon, Walt."

Wimberley went toward the livery barn, where he kept his team and rig. He debated about riding to his destination, then decided it would be warmer in a buggy — he could wrap a robe around his knees and thighs and keep warm. The hostler was out, evidently getting his supper, and the lawyer harnessed his team and hooked them to his buggy. It was an ornate affair, enclosed by side-curtains, with a strip of celluloid in the front panel, and through it he could see the team and the road. Also, there were slots in this panel for the reins to enter, and another allowed him to use his buggy-whip.

He did not drive down the main street, for he did not want to be seen leaving Singletree, but he went down the alley. As he passed the Broken Latigo, he heard the whine of Ponce de Leon Smith's violin; when he came around the corner, he glanced up the main street, noticing the lamp in Maggie Shaw's office. Evidently the husky woman was grinding out her special edition of *The Singletree Spy*.

Never one to underestimate anybody, ever on the alert, John Wimberley let his thoughts rest on Ponce de Leon Smith, then on Maggie Shaw. The former he finally dismissed as harmless to him and his work; the latter, he decided, would bear watching, and he would keep her and her sheet under close scrutiny. The persons he had to watch, though, and watch closely, were Judge Lemanuel Bates and Tobacco Jones, especially the judge.

Not for one moment, did he underestimate the jurist. He knew Judge Bates by reputation and by actual acquaintance, and he knew the jurist would be a tough foe, both in court and out, were he aroused. Judge Bates and Tobacco Jones had broken up the gun trap he and Val Marcus had set for Walt Gallatin. Now, driving through the evening, Attorney John Wimberley wondered if the judge suspected he was, and had been, an integral part of that nefarious, backfiring scheme.

He had decided, after long deliberation, to follow out two courses, lead where they might. One was to keep playing the game for Val Marcus; the other was to watch Judge Bates and Tobacco Jones.

The night was dark when he drove into the yard of the Rocking R. The roustabout took his team and the barrister got down, legs stiff and cold. The snow had stopped falling, but the wind still slung to its old chill. He pulled his sheepskin coat around his bony shoulders.

"The boss is in the house," the old man said.

There would be a warm stove and a smoke and a drink in the house, and the anticipation suddenly warmed John Wimberley, who dug into his pocket and got his wallet and gave the old-timer a silver dollar.

"Buy yourself a bottle, Ike."

Val Marcus was alone in the big room, shaving and squinting into the mirror, for his light was dull. He looked around, face half-covered with lather, the straight-edge razor in one hand, shaving-brush in the other.

"Well, I'll be damned. Wimberley, himself, on a night like this. Did they run you out of town on a rail?"

"Not yet, Val."

"Hope nobody saw you come out here."

Wimberley, warming his bony hands over the stove, assured him nobody had seen him drive to the Rocking R; the night was very dark, he had left Singletree by the back alley, he had stopped twice and scouted around to see if he were being followed. Did he have a drink?

Marcus waved his razor toward the desk, and Wimberley brought out a quart. He drank without a glass. Lew Basick came in from a side room, nodded briefly, settled in a chair, sitting beside the stove. Marcus, finally finished with his shaving, carried the wash-basin into the kitchen, where Wimberley heard him pour the water into the slop pail.

"Cold night?" Basick asked.

"Right smart night."

"You're forgettin' your high-toned language," Basick said. "You almost talk like a human sometimes."

Wimberley almost made a hot reply, but he held it in time. He hated Basick, and Basick hated him; he knew this.

Basick was a little jealous of him, resentful of his education and brains, and he, in turn, had taken to hate Basick, for the man's tongue was sharp. For that matter, he had no special love for Val Marcus, either. They were all wrapped in the same dark blanket. They were friends because of greed, not because of liking.

Marcus came back, rubbing his face with a towel. He stood beside the stove, massaging his face. John Wimberley was finally getting warm.

Marcus asked, "How do things set from your angle, John?"

Wimberley told him he still held the deeds belonging to Walt and Sarah Gallatin, but that Walt was getting impatient. He hoped to hold them until the three months were gone.

"I don't want him to get those deeds," Marcus said.

Basick cut in with, "I say give them the deeds, men. They might trace back, find out they were issued in Washington, and they might raise hob.

161

They could do that, couldn't they, John?"

Wimberley nodded.

But Marcus shook his head. "We'll have to chance that, men. I don't want them to get title to the land. They have to sign those deeds, don't they, and return them for recording?" Again, Wimberley nodded. "Well, if they don't come back, signed and all proper, they won't get those other homesteads, is that it?"

Wimberley cleared his throat. "That is right, Val."

Basick said, "Marcus, we ought to drift. We stay here, and we'll get picked up, sooner or later. We got the pile made. Let's pull out."

Marcus winked at Wimberley. "Lew's got cold boots. He's been walkin' too long in the snow. What else, John?"

Wimberley told about the arrival of Walt Gallatin's well-digging outfit. "It's on a flat-car down in the yards now. The crew will come in tomorrow, I understand. He'll get a well down, get water into irrigation ditches, and the farmers will come in like flies heading for a dead piece of horseflesh."

Marcus nodded.

Basick asked, "Well, Val?"

Marcus said, "When they get their casing down to water, we'll blow the well closed. We can't afford to let them get water on land we don't own."

Wimberley pointed out that, if the deeds were held up, Walt Gallatin would be broke, and would have to rip his fences up. He had already built ditches on the homesteads for which he and Sarah did not have deeds. He could not, under law, homestead these particular sections again. And Marcus intended to get men over there to take up these abandoned claims.

Marcus nodded, following the attorney's line of thought. "Then it would be a poor idea to blast out the well, huh? In fact, I'd be destroying property I could get for almost nothing, when Gallatin pulls out." He uncorked the bottle. "I'm goin' to proposition this gent that handles the well crew. Maybe I can get him to stall along, until three months are up — "

"Now you are talking." Wimberley encouraged him.

Basick pulled his bottom lip, deep in thought, scowling. Marcus studied him, unnoticed by the range boss, and Wimberley saw Marcus' face go stormy, hard as thunder on a mountain crag. For one moment, the man's strong, tough character lay bare, plain for the lawyer to see, and Wimberley, seeing this hardness, marked Val Marcus as extremely dangerous. Finally Basick caught Marcus' eyes and looked at him.

"What's wrong with you, Val?"

Marcus spoke very quietly and very pointedly. "Don't try to run out on me, Lew. Don't think of that."

Basick's white face showed a sudden blush, almost girlish. This left, and the skin lay white and bare, the eyes white, the pale eyebrows pulled down a little. "Are you a mind-reader, Marcus? Can you read my thoughts?"

"Sometimes I think so."

"I think different," Lew Basick stated.

John Wimberley built a pyramid out of his fingers and looked over this at Val Marcus, clearing his throat noisily. "Gentlemen, let us not delve into the mysteries of mind-reading and the future. I come for more important things than to hear you squabble. First, Marcus, call that man into the room."

"What man?"

"He's listening, in the next room."

Marcus studied the barrister, then called, "Mack, come in," and a blocky man entered, face dark with whiskers. He nodded, did not speak, but hunkered beside the stove, watching them, still silent.

Wimberley studied his fingers, now warm and pliable. Finally, talking in a low, certain voice, he told why he had come to the Rocking R, on such a night as this.

He had received a tip, he said, that the County of Winchester — three counties north and under the Montana Territorial line — would, in four days, receive some thirty thousand dollars in gold from the Denver mint. This gold would meet a payroll, for the county was engaged in some road-building, and was paying off in cash, for the workers would not tolerate the county warrants and their discount.

"Higham's the county seat, ain't it?" Marcus asked.

John Wimberley nodded. "Have you ever been there?"

Marcus smiled. "I spent a night in the clink there." He added, "That was about six years back."

Lew Basick smiled. Mac Byson stretched his leg, grinning a little. Even Lawyer John Wimberley allowed himself a small smile. From this information, then, Marcus would know the lay of the court-house, he reasoned. The money would come in the night of — here John Wimberley consulted a letter he had carried in his inner pocket — and would go immediately to the county clerk's office.

"I know where it is," Marcus said.

Byson said, "We already are spendin' it, lawyer."

There were other terms to be discussed. Their informer at the mint would have to be cut in, as usual; they all agreed to this, although Basick insisted he wanted too much, and his ante was getting higher and higher. Marcus disagreed with this, saying without him, and without Wimberley, where would they be? They all drank, the bottle going the rounds.

"Who is going north?" Wimberley wanted to know.

Marcus said Lew Basick and Mack Byson and another rider, maybe Blacky, would head for Higham. He would stay on Singletree Range. "Got things I need to tend to here," he said. "Besides, a bunch of the boys are comin' in in a few days. They got too hot in Colorado and are goin' lay low for a while. They're cuttin' us in on some raid money, too."

Wimberley smiled at that, and rubbed his bony hands. Basick said, "Is this all?" and Wimberley nodded. Basick left, his boots pounding down the hall, and Wimberley heard a door open and close. Marcus poured another drink, offered one to the lawyer, who shook his head.

Mack Byson got to his feet, an unshaven, uncouth rider, almost filthy, and Attorney John Wimberley, for one moment seeing the ugliness of the situation he was in, felt a sharp and useless tug of remorse. Byson drank loudly, wiped his mouth with the back of his hand, and looked at Wimberley.

"How did you know I was behind that door?"

Wimberley said, "I smelled you!"

12

SLEEP was a black blanket, wrapped around him securely, its darkness secure and warm. But now, piercing through this darkness, was the sound of knuckles on the door, the sound of a voice repeating. "Judge Bates, Judge Bates."

Judge Lemanuel Bates rolled over.

Sleep came in again, washing over him, but the knuckles, and the voice, pushed it aside rudely. Judge Lemanuel Bates sat up in bed.

The room was cold. Outside, the wind sang in the eaves as it scampered across the prairie. Tobacco Jones was snoring in the opposite bed.

"Who's there?"

"Me, the depot operator."

Judge Bates bade him enter, forgetting he had locked the door. The man reminded him of this fact, and down

169

the hall a man stuck his head out of a door to holler, "Put a hackamore on that jackass, somebody, or I'll bounce a pot off his long ears!"

"You'll do *what*?" the agent demanded.

By this time Judge Bates had crossed the room, the floor ice-cold on his bare feet, and he had unlocked the door. The agent was ready to turn down the hall, evidently eager to engage the wrathful roomer in a rough-and-tumble affair, but the jurist caught him by the shirt and jerked him into the room rather unceremoniously. The judge looked at the roomer, who stood in the hall in a flowing nightgown. He apologized, saying the agent was drunk.

"Too cold to argue, sir," he said. "A good night's rest to you, from here out."

"Darn near mornin' now," the roomer grumbled.

The judge closed the door. The agent had seated himself on a chair and, while the judge pokered the stove into life, the depot man rummaged in an inner pocket, evidently looking for something.

"I guess I lost it," he finally said.

Despite the ruckus, Tobacco Jones still snored on, his face to the wall and the bedding heaped over him. And the judge, moving closer to the stove, saw that his first surmise was correct. The depot agent was not drunk; he was saturated.

"Ol' lady left today for a two-week visit with her mother in Cheyenne. My ol' girl came up from Lander to celebrate with me. Dang it, Bates, I can't find that message."

"Maybe it's in your other pocket."

Tobacco Jones sat up suddenly, blinking at the lamplight. "What the snakes is goin' on, Bates?"

"We're going on a snipe hunt, Tobacco."

Tobacco stuck his knuckles into his eyes and yawned. "Amen, it's cold in here. What a hotel!" He studied the agent, who still was looking in his pockets. "What happened to junior? His mammy kick him off the spread?"

"He's got a message," the judge replied.

Tobacco rolled back into his bedding, again facing the wall. "You get messages day an' night," he grumbled. "I'm glad I'm not important."

The judge was getting colder and more impatient.

"I was crossin' the street, Bates, weavin' my way along, an' this danged lawyer almost run over me, comin' down the street in that high-falutin' rig of his'n, all side-curtains an' window-glass. I jumped, but he danged near run his off-hoss over me. I swore him out, but he just stuck his head out and told me I was drunk, which I reckon I was. I might've lost the message then."

The judge wondered why Attorney Wimberley, or any other honest man, would be out at such an hour in such weather, and then he decided that maybe John Wimberley was not as honest as he proclaimed by his pious mien and upright carriage. But he made no mention of this to the agent.

"Here it is," the agent cried triumphantly.

From an inner pocket he took out a mangled yellow piece of paper, the kind messages are inscribed upon. He started to unfold this, fingers moving in drunken clumsiness, but the jurist, tired of this fooforaw, took the paper and did the chore himself, holding it close to the light to read it. But the creased paper made difficult reading.

"I'll need my glasses."

"Try mine, Bates."

The agent fairly crammed the glasses down on the judge's nose. The words looked as big as horse hoofs, the intense magnification making the judge a little tipsy. He handed back the glasses, got his own from the bed-stand, and read aloud to Tobacco, who had rolled over and was listening —

"Judge Lemanuel Bates:

Pursuant recent telegram, have collected from one box-car, heading out of Wyoming, one gentleman answering to description of old Potter, who says, too, his name is Jim Potter. Said Potter now resides in my calaboose. What do with him? Clonked on head, he claims, and woke up on box-car. Who hit him? He does not know. Cooking supper, he said, and walked out to swear at dog, then his lamp went out. He stinks up jail. Send fare for return?
    Sheriff Tim O'Maloney,
    Twin Buttes, Wyoming."

"Wonder what happened?" the agent asked.

Tobacco was scowling, the judge frowning. "We'll send him return fare in the morning," he said. "How far is it to Twin Buttes?"

After frowning deeply and counting on his fingers, the agent allowed Twin

174

Buttes was about a hundred miles distant, and that, if old Potter had been knocked out, somebody had done a thorough job. No, he'd keep this information to himself; he wouldn't even tell his lady friend.

"But that is collect," he reminded Bates.

The judge dug into his pants, coming out with the required sum.

Somebody came up the stairs, lurching and making a lot of noise, and a shrill feminine voice hollered shrilly, "Hey, Elmer, where are ye? This is Honey Love hollerin' to you!"

"In here, Honey!"

Tobacco said, "Heave him out, Bates, or she'll wake up the joint, and they'll want to kill us!" He was out of bed now, at Elmer's other elbow, hazing the agent down the hall. Honey stood at the foot of the stairs, seemingly braced against a strong wind, and she came running ahead, her gait broken and unsteady.

"Elmer, I thought maybe your wife

had come back an' nabbed you! You scared me, Elmer."

Doors were popping open, up and down the cold hall. They looked grotesque in the dim light of the dawn. Curses spewed forth, directed toward four drunken louts, and Tobacco Jones, being accused of drinking, got angry indeed. But the jurist, taking command, implored his partner to control himself.

"Where's the landlord?" a bull-throated man hollered. "Throw this drunken mess out on the street, or I will."

Honey and Elmer were arm in arm. They came to the top of the stairs, started down, and Elmer fell, dragging Honey down. The landlord, a tall, bony man, stood at the foot of the stairs, dressed in red underwear. He caught the agent and pulled him upright.

"My friend, too," he said.

The agent stood up, and Honey got to her feet. "I skinned my knee," she said. The landlord escorted them to the door, still shaking his head. They went outside, and Judge Bates and Tobacco Jones returned to their room. By this time, most of the roomers had pulled their heads back, but the bull-throated fellow still had his head sticking out.

"You drunks ain't leavin', eh? I oughta heave you out, breakin' up a man's rest."

Tobacco stopped, Judge Bates tugged at him, got him moving. Bull-Throat followed them down the hall, asking for trouble. He followed them to their door. Judge Bates stopped.

"My good man, are you a human fog-horn?"

"Don't 'good man' me," the fellow said angrily. "If you want to know, short man, I'm a salesman."

"Go home," the judge advised.

The salesman put his hands on his hips, regarding them belligerently. The judge, having had enough, was just ready to hit him on the button when the landlord came up the stairs.

"Mr. Shay, start no trouble here."

The man was out of breath. "I'm sorry, men, that my night clerk was asleep, otherwise that drunk and his woman would never have got to disturb you, Judge Bates."

The salesman said hollowly, "Judge Bates." He turned and left, and the judge winked at Tobacco, who grinned.

13

VAL MARCUS pounded into the office of *The Singletree Spy*, with Lew Basick a step behind him. Maggie Shaw was at her desk, proof-reading an advertisement. Marcus said, "I guess you're editor, reporter, and printer here, ain't you?"

Maggie's pencil made a correction. "I am, unless the sheriff has foreclosed on me in the last minute." She looked up at the Rocking R owner and his range boss. "What's on your mind beside your hat, Mr. Marcus."

Marcus had a wrinkled copy of *The Spy*. He unspread the four-page tabloid-type paper on Maggie's desk. "Did you write that, Mrs. Shaw?"

The woman glanced at the editorial. "Yes, I did. In fact, I wrote the whole paper." She leaned her heavy body back against her chair, the swivel-spring creaking under her pressure. "I judge from your manner, you did not like my editorial, Marcus."

"I don't," Marcus said.

Lew Basick watched unblinkingly.

Maggie Shaw's shrewd, dark eyes looked up at the angry Rocking R owner. "I write the way it looks to me, sir. And from my viewpoint, you are holding up the progress of Singletree Range. You and your gunmen are keeping farmers from settling here, and on the farmers' shoulders — and not the cattlemen — is the fate of Wyoming. You cattlemen have had your chance. You muffed it."

"I don't think so," Marcus said steadily.

"I do."

Basick finally spoke. "A matter of personal opinion, madam." He looked long at the press, at the pile of paper, at the hell-box with its scattered type. He even looked at the floor.

Marcus said, "You don't scare, Mrs. Shaw."

180

"Not worth a damn, sir."

Basick had finally brought his gaze back to *The Spy*'s editor. Maggie thought, 'I wonder what he's thinking about?' and realized that the pale eyes showed nothing. Lew Basick wet his lips and was silent.

Val Marcus tried new tactics. "Mrs. Shaw, I have a proposition to make, one I think you'll be interested in."

Talking quietly, he outlined his plan. She would throw her paper behind him and the Rocking R, building public opinion to favor him and his cause, and he, in return, would put her on the Rocking R payroll. Lew Basick listened, still dead-pan, and this time he wondered what thoughts Maggie Shaw had, for her eyes were without life.

"Three hundred per month," Marcus said.

The coils of dark hair showed negation as Maggie shook her head slowly.

Marcus added, "Three-fifty."

Again, a slow shake.

"Four hundred."

"No, sir."

Marcus said, a little angry, "That's as high as I'll ante, woman." He was a little bit at a loss, dealing with a woman this way. Up to now, he had dealt with men, and sometimes you could use force against a man; but you could not use force against a woman.

"That's plenty high, Mr. Marcus."

Marcus smiled.

"I could never make four hundred a month from *The Spy*, even if I were flooded with job work, which I won't be in a town this size. I could never hope to clear even three hundred per month. Your offer, sir, was very liberal." The woman stood up, hands on her desk. "Nobody can accuse you of being a cheapskate." She looked at Marcus, then at Basick. Then she said, "Now both of you get out of here." She added, "And stay out!"

Marcus said, "Think it over, woman."

"I've thought it over. Get out!"

"Don't jump the tugs," Marcus warned. Nevertheless, he started toward the door, his anger scawled across his loose lips. He stopped at the door, for Basick was speaking, his words very dry.

"Mrs. Shaw, a number of printing establishments have been mysteriously blown up, you know."

"Don't threaten me, you thief."

Marcus said, "Come on, Lew."

Basick turned, bleakness on his pale face, and followed his boss outside. Maggie Shaw watched them go, and now her hands, resting flat on the desk, showed a sudden tremble through the big knuckles. So that was why that Basick dog was so carefully casing the place? He was figuring where he'd place his dynamite to do the most damage!

She decided, from now on, to sleep in the office. She would let this word get around, and they would not dare dynamite with her inside. She would also put out a special edition, although it would only be a column or two, telling the local people she had already been threatened, but she decided not to name Marcus and Basick as the principals involved. She had no proof that they had threatened her. Had she had a witness to listen in —

Tobacco Jones came in and said, "Mrs. Shaw, you look pale. You eat somethin' that don't agree with you?"

She told him about Marcus' and Basick's visit. Tobacco chewed, listening, and she came closer than he intended; the first thing he knew, she had both arms around his neck, and was weeping on his shoulder. The Cowtrail postmaster didn't know just what to do. He couldn't get away — for she held him too tightly — and he decided he would just weather the storm as best he could. He patted her on the back, and decided she had a back as wide as a small saddle-horse.

"Don't cry, Maggie. Hang onto your nerves."

"I'm scared."

The postmaster chewed and scowled, patting methodically all the time. He was getting very embarrassed. He knew that Maggie Shaw was not as nervous as she let on; she had just seen a chance — and the opportunity — to put her arms around him. Just then, Judge Bates entered.

The jurist, carrying his jug, stopped inside the door, and Tobacco Jones, looking over Maggie's shoulder, saw an amused smile on his lips. Evidently Maggie had not heard the judge enter.

The judge winked at Tobacco, held his fingers across his lips, then started tiptoeing out again. Tobacco, feeling a moment of panic, said hoarsely, "Don't leave, hey!"

Maggie did not look around. "Who are you talking to?"

"My wife."

Maggie released him instantly. She said, "Blast you!" and stepped back. Then she saw the judge. "Come on in, Judge Bates." Then, to Tobacco: "I thought you were single."

"I am. And I inten' to stay just that way."

Maggie wiped her eyes with a handkerchief she had on her desk. "I guess I was just nervous — and sick, Judge Bates." She told about the visit of Lew Basick and Val Marcus and her decision to sleep in her office to keep the Rocking R pair from blowing it up. Judge Bates nodded, said her decision was good, and also urged her to print her contemplated extra.

"But let me read it in proof, first, Madam. I am, as you know, an authority on libel."

"You can't know more about libel than I do, Judge Bates. I've been sued so many times I know the libel law better than most lawyers."

Now that he was free, Tobacco Jones kept a good distance from Maggie, and the woman, noticing this, glared at him, but he only grinned. The judge and postmaster went to the depot, where they sent a message to Sheriff Tim O'Maloney at Twin Buttes, guaranteeing fare for old Potter's return to Singletree. Elmer had evidently not recovered from his spree, and a kid ran the key. He tapped out the message and then waited for a reply.

"They're unloadin' Walt Gallatin's well-diggin' rig," Tobacco said. "Let's mosey down an' look it over, eh, Bates?"

They walked against the harsh, cold wind. The well-digging crew was at work unloading its apparatus into two wagons. Val Marcus and Lew Basick stood and watched the men work, the well-crew foreman standing beside Marcus.

The judge glanced at the foreman, a red-haired, big-shouldered gent wearing bib-overalls, a flannel shirt and calk boots. Green-grey eyes met the judge's glance, then flicked back to where two men were lifting on the well-bit.

"Better get some help with that, men," the foreman said. "That's hard to handle alone."

Judge Bates noticed the foreman

made no move to help his men. Finally, they got the bit onto a wagon. Marcus and Basick watched the men work, too.

"Looks like a good outfit." Judge Bates wanted to start conversation rolling, just to see what reaction the Rocking R men would have toward the well-digging outfit and its crew.

"Looks all right," Marcus said.

Basick was silent.

Judge Bates said, "Get water on this land, Marcus, and it'll be like a garden; this soil will raise anything that will grow in this climate — when it gets water on it."

"I reckon so," Marcus said.

The jurist glanced at his partner, noticing Tobacco Jones' scowl as he masticated his tobacco. He had expected to get a rise out of the hot-tempered Rocking R owner, but for some reason he had failed. And that didn't seem logical. The jurist tried a new tactic.

"Heard you two threatened Maggie Shaw for printing that editorial about you?"

Marcus looked at him, his gaze cold and long. Basick seemed interested in the well-digging equipment, but the judge knew the gun-hand was only seeking a pretense — inside, he was tough and vigilant. Finally Marcus smiled.

"Women always talk too much, Bates."

Basick said: "They do that."

The Rocking R pair turned and walked toward the main street. Judge Bates pushed back his hat, rubbed his forehead thoughtfully, and then looked inquiringly at his partner. "They're almost congenial," he said. "And I don't see why."

"Neither do I."

They introduced themselves to the foreman, who turned out to be named Nels Tanhill. According to Tanhill, young Walt had stepped downtown for a moment, and would be back soon. Who were those two gents that had just left?

For some reason, the judge figured Tanhill had been introduced to Marcus and Basick, but evidently he was wrong. So he told about the two Rocking R men and how they would be against getting the well punched down to water. At this, Nels Tanhill smiled, and said his men were tough; they had come in to put down a well, and the well would go down, Marcus or no Marcus.

"That's the talk, sir."

The judge uncorked his jug and Nels Tanhill drank noisily. Walt Gallatin came up, carrying a length of new three-quarter-inch rope he had just purchased at the Mercantile; they would tie down the load with it. He and the jurist talked for a while and then Tobacco and the judge went back to the depot. The kid was just transcribing the last of Sheriff O'Maloney's message.

Judge Bates read:

"Prisoner will not leave jail. Has struck up friendship with cell-mate. Tried to throw him out but could not.

What next?

Sheriff Tim O'Maloney, Twin Buttes, Wyoming."

"Is he loco?" Tobacco marveled.

Judge Bates scowled and re-read the message. There was no other conclusion to draw, he figured: old Potter had gone crazy. He had climbed on a freight, pulled out, and concocted a cock-and-bull story about being slugged.

"What're we going to do, Bates?"

Judge Bates shrugged. "What can we do?" He answered his own question. "Just leave him there. If he is crazy, the courts will so ascertain; he will be locked up. But he always seemed logical to me, the few times I met him."

"Me, too."

"Funny world," the judge murmured. They were turning to leave when the

191

operator said, "Another message, sir."
He handed the jurist the paper.

"Prisoner just escaped. Broke out of bull-pen with cell-mate, wanted for drunkenness. Heading for Winchester County, reports say. Will let drunkenness charge drop. But what about your man?

Sheriff Tim O'Maloney,
Twin Buttes, Wyoming."

Tobacco rubbed his jaw thoughtfully. "Seems to me like that lawman sounds glad to get shut of both of them, Bates. Maybe he helped them pull out, eh?"

The judge allowed this had been done before. He'd turned loose a few prisoners himself, with their promise they would get out of his bailiwick. The whole thing was crazy, he decided. Better drop it, tell the Gallatins old Potter was gone and let it go at that.

"Any answer?" the kid asked.

The judge scribbled, 'Sheriff O'Maloney, forget Potter case,' and handed it to the youth, who rattled his key so quickly it made an incessant blur. They went outside.

"Nutty world," Tobacco murmured.

The judge reminded him the world was all right, but sometimes a man got to thinking the people who inhabited it were all loco. "But don't worry, Tobacco. Five billion years from now, geologists say, the ice-cap will come back, making men extinct on this globe."

"How many years, Bates?"

"Five billion."

Tobacco bit off a chew. "You had me scared for a while, Judge. I thought at first you'd said only five *million*!"

14

VAL MARCUS and Lew Basick went into the Broken Latigo Saloon, where they had a drink. Marcus smiled a little and said, "Smokey, drink with us?"

Smokey watched him. "After our ruckus the other day?"

"We had too much to drink," Marcus said. "A bunch of fools, walkin' with six-shooters in our hands."

Smokey poured. "Here's to you, Marcus."

They all drank. The two Rocking R men walked out to the broncs, spurs making sounds, and Maggie Shaw came along the street. Marcus lifted his hat and said, "Hello, Honey. How's the writing business?"

Maggie stopped, eyes shrewd. Finally, "Sometimes you're almost human, Marcus."

Marcus looked hard at her. "We *could* get along fine," he said. He found his stirrup and lifted his weight. Basick was in saddle, lithe and colorless, and they rode down the street, broncs single-footing. Basick said, "The wind is behind us . . . for once," and seemed to find satisfaction in that.

They rode for a mile, Singletree falling behind.

Basick asked, "Have we got it all covered, Val? Can you see a loophole? Can you see where they'd get us?"

"What do you think, Lew?"

Basick was silent. At last, "I've run over it . . . time an' time again. I can't see a knothole, Val."

"Neither can I."

Basick looked back at Singletree, now almost hidden behind the jutting of the huge talus cone that came down from the mountains. The wind was sharp against him, drawing his face down into lines, and these lines left as he looked back at Marcus and said, "Judge Bates."

Marcus lifted his shoulders under his sheepskin. "A cagey man, but what can he suspect?"

"He knows about Wimberley's past record. He's bound to know that."

"Yes, but he doesn't know Wimberley is associated with us, Lew."

Basick pondered that. "John Wimberley is too careless. He's glib, with a smart tongue; his brain is a double-bitted sharp axe. And because he's smart, he takes too many chances."

"We've got to have him, though."

Basick looked up at the snow-tipped peaks. "There's a warm country beyond those. You hit the desert and cross it and then the mountains. There's Frisco, there's Santa Barbara, there's San Diego."

Marcus reminded him, "I've seen them, too."

"Sometimes a man feels big inside, Marcus. He feels like building big things, tearing down high mountains. Then suddenly he feels small and weak; I guess he feels the way he really is."

Marcus had no answer. There were times when he did not understand Lew Basick, and there were times he did not understand himself; this was one of those times.

They put their ponies to a lope, letting the miles drift behind them. Rocking R cattle grazed on the sidehills and in coulees; Marcus looked at them, and liked them. They were good stock. They were fat stock.

Marcus found himself smiling. "A man sure is crazy, Lew. Here we got a good outfit — buildings, saddle-stock, range. What if the farmers did come in? They'd settle the bottoms, raise crops, hay. Where one ton of wild bluejoint grows now, a good farmer'd raise four ton of alfalfa.

"We could run our stuff back in the hills, buy hay from the farmers, feed good winters. Cheaper than us cutting a poor hay-crop, and we'd raise tougher, fatter cattle. We'd still have plenty of grass come summer, too."

"But there'd be no trouble," Basick said, smiling.

"Too darn peaceful, Lew."

They ran into the Rocking R, the buildings seeming calm and peaceful, there on the bottom. They unstripped their sweaty broncs and tied them in stalls in the log barn. Here the wind would not hit them and they could dry off before going into pasture.

Wimberley awaited them in the house. He was sitting beside the fire, his gaunt torso bent at the waist, his bony hands clasped together as he looked at the fire in the rock fireplace. He seemed to be entranced by the fire. He did not look up when they came in.

Marcus said, "We figured you'd be here, Wimberley. We were in the Broken Latigo, and we heard a man say you'd left your office."

"Don't inquire about me," Wimberley spoke darkly. He kept looking at the fire. "We don't want to be seen together too much, Marcus."

Marcus murmured. "You don't need to tell me."

Something in the cowman's tone brought the lawyer's eyes away from the fire to Marcus and Basick. Something inside, some errant, unknown thought, brought a smile to the lawyer's thin lips.

"Mrs. Shaw talked to me, sirs."

Marcus grinned boyishly. "I jumped over my tugs, John. I'll turn around and let you boot me. I tried the tough method; I wanted to see if she would scare. She won't scare. Then I tried to buy her. She won't sell. She's an odd character. She won't scare, she won't sell."

Basick asked, "What did she want?"

John Wimberley told them that Maggie Shaw had retained him as her attorney, giving him a retainer fee. He had tried to talk her out of running the second editorial, and he had failed. Marcus smiled at this information.

"Let her run it, John. We want this basin kept in a turmoil. We want the local citizens to be wrapped up in so much trouble, they won't bother to think of trouble in other parts of the territory. Now we got her where we want her; spark her a little bit, and she'll fall for you."

"I got a wife," Wimberley said, still smiling.

Basick asked bluntly, "You have? Where is she?"

Wimberley waved a bony hand in a gesture denoting great time and great distance. Then he laughed, head back. "Sure, I'll play up to her, men. Without her knowing it, I'll have her running my editorial policy, not hers. But how about Judge Bates and Tobacco Jones?"

Basick repeated, "How about them?"

Marcus stood, scowling. He walked to the fire, held out his hands, warmed them. "We take each thing as it comes up. There's no use rushing ahead on guess-work. I wonder what became of old Potter?"

They all wondered about that. It

seemed odd, Wimberley remarked, that old Potter hadn't come back. Basick said, with a little haste, that maybe the old man had died in the box-car. Then he reassured himself by the remark that, had Potter died, surely his body would have been found, and identified, by now.

"He mighta got so scared he jus' kept on travellin," Val Marcus stated. "He might've got rabbity an' pulled out for good, afraid that the next time would be the last time."

"What difference does it make?" Wimberley wanted to know.

Marcus got a bottle from the chiffonier and it went its rounds. They talked about Judge Bates and Tobacco Jones and even mentioned Ponce de Leon Smith. Wimberley steered the conversation around to Winchester County up north.

"Where's Mack Byson?"

Byson had drifted back into the timber, Marcus said; he did not want to stay around the Rocking R; somebody might see him and recognize him. He was camped up under the rimrock off Black Butts. Wimberley nodded, saying this was a good move, and he made other inquiries. Who was going north to Higham with Basick?

Basick answered that. Byson would go, of course, and they'd pick up a man up north, and then another closer to Higham. Byson had the thing lined up; he had his men stationed. They'd make the divvy later on, if the hold-up went through successfully. It all depended on things working smoothly up in Winchester County.

"Things will go through all right," Wimberley said.

Basick said scoffingly, "Sure, that's nice to say, fella. But if an' when the guns boom, you'll be settin' in a warm office, feet on the stove-rail. Lew Basick and Mack Byson will be in the powder-smoke, though."

"Brains pays off, Basick."

Basick had his fists doubled. For once, something cracked inside of him, and Marcus, watching him, saw something for the first time — and this something was the terrible, strong hate Basick held for John Wimberley. He had guessed at it, but now he saw its terrible strength.

Marcus said quietly, "Lew, hold down."

Wimberley had his hand in his coat pocket. Marcus looked at that hand, saw the hard outline against the suit pocket, and he said again, speaking almost like a father, "Lew, listen to me."

Wordlessly, Basick turned his gaze on Marcus. He looked long at the Rocking R boss, eyes without thoughts, and for a moment, he seemed miles away, facing something that neither Wimberley or Marcus could imagine. Then he said, "All right, friend," and turned and walked out of the room, his boot-heels running down the hall and dying in direct ratio to distance.

A door closed, silence.

Only then did John Wimberley

draw back his hand. He said, "He's breaking," and he looked at Marcus, who only shook his head. Wimberley repeated, "He's coming apart, Marcus."

"You don't know him, John."

Wimberley waited, patient.

Marcus said, "When he's that way — tight as a rawhide catch-rope — when he's like that, he's dangerous. It'll grow on him between here an' Higham, an' when the test comes, it leaves him. He'll be steel, then, until it's over; then he'll look for something hard to drink."

"He'd better not move against me."

Marcus slowly uncorked the whisky bottle. "John, did you ever hear of a law that could turn a bullet? You got the law on your side, but he's got the bullet, and it's a mighty fast bullet, too."

"The law is stronger."

"Not when a man's dead, it ain't." Marcus saw that Wimberley's hand trembled as he reached for the bottle. "But drink, friend, and forget this.

Come an hour, Lew Basick will have forgotten. But don't rub his fur wrong again, eh?"

They talked of many things: the deeds belonging to Walt and Sarah Gallatin, and Marcus told how he had accosted Nels Tanhill, the drill boss. "I felt him out, John, and we'll make arrangements, I'm dang sure. He doesn't care what the casing looks like; he likes the looks of money."

"Who doesn't?"

Wimberley stayed until dusk. By evening the wind had fallen and, when it was getting dark, the lawyer got his saddle horse out of the brush and rode back toward his office in Singletree.

He rode at a walk, still remembering the threat of Lew Basick. From now on out, he'd walk light around Basick, and he'd have his gun handy. This game was dangerous, freighted with peril, and it was a checkerboard, with its men scattered around. He ran over the moves in his mind, checking and rechecking, looking ahead.

He was methodical.

Once he stopped, horse hidden in buckbrush, and he watched a rider below him. He had just glimpsed the man as he rode between two clumps of cottonwoods. He never saw him again.

He thought, A Rocking R rider, heading home.

He found the wagon road and put his pony to a lope. But, for some reason, he kept remembering that stranger he'd seen; he was, in a vague, nebulous way, a familiar figure —

But still he could not place him.

15

JUDGE BATES was worried.

Boots on his desk, he sat in his office, back pushing hard against his swivel chair, hands laced across his belly. His jug sat on the desk corner within reach. His blue suit was draped across his wide shoulders and his hat, hanging from the rawhide jaw thongs, lay across the back of his chair.

He didn't look worried, though.

For one thing, his heavy face was without a scowl, and his eyes were lidded, hiding what thoughts eyes are supposed to portray. But he wasn't asleep. His mind was reaching out, dragging in thoughts, mulling over them. He was searching for something.

There were a number of angles to consider.

One was, where were the deeds

belonging to Walt and Sarah Gallatin? They should have been filed, sent for signature, and been returned for recording. But so far they hadn't been returned.

Another was, what was Ponce de Leon Smith — and the monkey, Alexander — doing on Singletree Range?

To the first question, the answer could be gained by wiring to the Bureau of Interior in Washington, D.C. To the second there seemed no visible answer.

Boots came down the hall, registering their dull sounds and Bates guessed at their owner's identity from the sound of the heels. And the voice, coming from the doorway, gave positive evidence his surmisals had been correct.

"I understan', Judge Bates, that ol' Potter busted outa the Twin Butte jail, eh?"

The judge did not look around. "Who informed you thus, Sheriff Bennett?"

Rube Bennett's lanky form angled into the room, stopped beside the window. "Looks like winter's here," the lawman declared. Then, "The kid down the depot tol' me."

Judge Bates said, "He is violating the law, sir, by giving the information received in telegrams."

Rube Bennett looked at him. "Why didn't you tell me about ol' Potter? I've been lookin' for him, too. My office has been worried; I've had deputies out ridin', figurin' he might've wandered off, drunk, an' kicked the bucket somewhere. After all, I'm the law here, Judge."

"That's right, you are."

Bennett didn't know how to take that. "You got your boots on thet county desk, Bates. You done tol' me once that was wrong to do. Defacin' county property, you said."

Judge Bates reminded the sheriff that he had no spurs to dig into the desk. Evidently Sheriff Rube Bennett was in an irritable mood.

"Wife rough on you, Sheriff?"

Bennett rubbed his hands together. "Reckon you've heard about my missus too, eh? Yeah, she's a wildcat with rubber tires, Bates. If'n it weren't for my kids, I'd hightail out." He reflected, his long face grave. "No, maybe not. She's a good cook, with all her faults."

There was a silence.

"Think Marcus has enough evidence to convict Gallatin?"

"I don't know."

Another silence.

"Hope not. I like Sary."

"Good girl."

Another silence.

Finally Sheriff Bennett said, "See you later, Judge," and left. He went into his office and slammed the door. More boots came; the judge guessed again; again he was right.

Tobacco Jones asked, "Asleep, Bates?"

The judge got up. "Let's go to the depot." They went down the street. Frost rimmed windows; hung to leafless boughs. Elmer was at work. The judge asked where the kid was, and Elmer said he'd caught the passenger train out an hour before. He'd gone back to the home office in Cheyenne.

"Why ask about him, Bates?"

The judge stated that the kid had revealed to Sheriff Bennett the contents of a telegram concerning old Potter. Elmer clucked, said that was against the rules; he'd notify the home office. "Prob'ly can the kid, too."

"Don't notify them, then."

Elmer grinned. "Sheriff Bennett ain't got sense enough to remember what the kid told him, nowhere or nohow."

The jurist offered Elmer a drink. The agent declined with many gestures. Judge Bates drank and left his jug sitting on the counter. Elmer eyed it, said his head felt as if it were full of dust.

"Have a snort of it, Elmer. Sample the hair of the dog that bit you."

Finally Elmer took a short drink. He breathed with great gusto, and claimed the whisky hadn't tasted too rough, at that; he took another drink. He got into a patronizing mood.

"Somethin' I kin do for you, Judge Bates?"

The judge was scribbling on a telegram blank. The pen caught and made ink splotches. "Yes, you can give me your soft-leaded pencil, sir." The pencil worked better. Tobacco read over the jurist's shoulder.

"Homestead Department,
U.S. Department of Interior,
Washington, D.C.
Sirs:
Re claims of Walt and Sarah Gallatin, Singletree Township, Territory of Wyoming. Said deeds have never been received by the Gallatins, and deeds are due. Land description will follow if necessary. Appreciate quick reply.

Judge Lemanuel Bates,
Acting County Judge,
Singletree, Wyoming."

"That ought to get some action, Judge," Tobacco stated.

The jurist re-read his message and put the pencil against his bottom lip thoughtfully. "But the federal offices are slow. I hope they can get me an answer without wiring back for the description of the land in question. If they want the descriptions, we'll have to get them from the assessor's files, and wire them back." He handed the message to Elmer. "Remember, sir, this is strictly confidential; not a word of this is to leak out of your office."

"I got two years, six months, twelve days and — " here Elmer glanced at the clock " — six minutes and five seconds until I get my pension, Judge Bates. For the last ten years the railroad company have had men hanging around, spotters hopin' to catch me short, so they can can me without payin' my pension. The closer I get to my pension, the more spotters drop by to check up on me."

"They've probably paid more out to spotters than your pension'll come to."

Tobacco unpeeled the tinfoil from a fresh plug of Horseshoe. "I judge that by your drinking, sir. Make another trip up to our room, drunk like that, and if whisky doesn't strike you dead, some irate roomer will."

"Heard that prune hound wanted to fight with you gents." Elmer walked to his key, reading the message. He tapped it through, eyes on the copy, and then hung up his head phones. "I'll notify you the minute an answer comes in, Bates."

Judge Bates thanked him and the partners turned to go. The key started to click and Elmer listened to the call, then said suddenly, "Wait a minute, men. A message for you."

The message didn't make sense. It was crazy. It was weird. It came from a cow-town in the northern part of the Territory, and even its point of origin was crazy. It came from Ten Cows, Wyoming.

The judge read it twice.

"Judge Lemanuel Bates,
Mr. Tobacco Jones,
Singletree, Wyoming.

Friends and enemies:
By these presents, let me tell you
I am going to Higham.
                                    Potter."

The judge said, "I don't savvy it."

Tobacco Jones grunted, "He's crazy, that's all. What do we care if he does go to Higham? 'Friends and enemies,' he says. 'By these presents,' he says. His cinch-ring is galling his brain, if he has one. He must've slipped his mental picket-pin an' wandered off."

The judge was silent.

Elmer looked at the jurist's jug, opened his mouth, noticed the judge's intense interest in the telegram. He just reached over and got the jug and uncorked it and drank. His eyes, Tobacco Jones noticed, had queer, sharp lights in them. He decided that

Elmer was on the way again.

Tobacco repeated, "He's loco."

"I don't agree, Jones."

The postmaster snorted. "What do we care if he goes to Higham, Bates? An' why didn't he wire to Walt Gallatin, 'stead of us? He's Walt's friend, an' just an acquaintance of ours."

"You said something, then."

Elmer reached again for the jug, but the jurist's fat hand came down on his wrist. "Don't hit it too hard, friend. You want to finish your shift, don't you? You owe that to the railroad."

"I don't owe this outerfit nothin', Bates."

Judge Bates pocketed the telegram. The partners went to the courthouse, and to the stove in the jurist's legal chambers. Tobacco was grumbling, a habit he had when pressed by difficulties, but the judge's heavy face was bland as he nodded to acquaintances, which included one John Wimberley, a local legal light.

"A beautiful fall day," Wimberley declared.

The judge said it was, indeed. Tobacco mumbled that it would be nicer if the sun was hotter. He didn't like the slick-eared shyster; neither, for that matter, did Judge Lem Bates. The only difference was that the judge, polished and suave when the occasion demanded, could hide his dislike under a cloak of easy formality; Tobacco did not possess this attribute.

"I am going to see my client, Mrs. Shaw."

Judge Bates' eyebrows lifted.

"Mrs. Shaw had a run-in with the Rocking R, with Marcus and Basick. I am protecting her legal interests and acting as an advisor to her in editorial policy."

"She left herself unprotected, sir, in that second editorial and Marcus certainly would have grounds for a libel suit and win it."

Wimberley's sad eyes were unblinking. "That is a matter of personal opinion,

Judge Bates. Good day, sirs."

John Wimberley crossed the street, heading for the office of *The Singletree Spy*, where, through the big front window, the partners could see Maggie Shaw, whose strong right arm was working the handle of the flat-bed press. Judge Bates was grunting something that sounded like "I'd like to get one of Wimberley's cases up in court," and Tobacco said, "Don't pay no 'tention to that gas-bag, Bates. If you do, you'll get as crazy as he is."

"Don't underestimate Wimberley, partner. He is far from crazy, I can assure you."

Tobacco smiled. "Well, he'll take Maggie off my shoulders anyway. She's just lookin' for some man to put out his shoulder to bawl on." He smiled more broadly. "She'll have her arms around Wimberley right smart, you can bet."

"You sound jealous."

"Jealous! You gone loco, Bates?"

Ponce de Leon Smith stood on the corner, sawing on his violin.

Alexander, chattering with the cold, sat in the gutter, using the curb for protection. The monkey spied Judge Bates, squealed in delight, and ran up the judge's suit, finally arriving on the jurist's wide shoulder, where he put his arms around the thick neck and pressed his cold mouth against the blue-shaven jowl.

The judge, finding satisfaction in the monkey's apparent adoration for him, stroked the little fellow's wiry fur, and Alexander chattered all the time, acting as though he were telling some intimate secret to the judge. Ponce de Leon Smith stopped fiddling, and Tobacco Jones was glad of that.

"Why, Judge Bates and Mr. Jones. How are you, sirs?"

"How did you know we was us?" Tobacco wanted to know.

Ponce de Leon Smith explained. For one thing, by now he could recognize the sound of their boots, for each man, he said, walked differently. For another thing, Alexander had run to

Judge Bates; never, in the years he had had the animal, had Alexander fallen so completely into friendship with anybody but himself.

"How goes things?" the judge asked.

Ponce de Leon Smith answered this question after some deliberation. He was barely making an income; plainly it was time to move to another town. Perhaps he would go south for the winter, possibly to New Orleans, where the climate was better adapted to his limited wardrobe. Yes, he would leave Singletree soon; his work, he said, was done here.

The judge invited him into the Broken Latigo for a drink.

It was warm inside the saloon. Smokey was alone, dozing beside the stove, and the judge, at a nod from the saloonman, went behind the bar, where he poured two drinks, set the opened quart on the mahogany, and came around the end again. He lifted his glass.

"To your future luck, sir."

"I'll need it, Judge Bates."

The judge asked further discreet questions. How did Ponce de Leon travel between towns? The beggar said he usually caught passenger trains, unless some good soul gave him a ride with a rig. "I cannot climb on a freight, sirs, for without my eyes — "

The judge glanced at Tobacco. Tobacco, seeing method to the judge's questioning, remained silent, chewing and scowling. Smokey kept on dozing.

The entrance of young Walt Gallatin broke up the conversation. Walt had a drink, then went upstairs to Wimberley's office. Fifteen minutes later he came down. Judge Bates asked, "Did those deeds come yet?"

"No sign of them, John says. Where t'hades are they? What kind of an office force have they got in Washington, anyway?"

The judge admitted it was odd they had not arrived by now.

"I wanted to wire Washington," Walt Gallatin said, "But Wimberley said he had already wired them four times, so there was no use in me wiring them."

The judge switched the conversation to the well-digging. The crew was going to work, Gallatin said; it would be extra work for Sarah, though, cooking for all those men. Old Potter had been some help in the kitchen, but old Potter had run out. He had been heard of in Twin Buttes.

"Well, he isn't dead then," said the judge.

Gallatin said he had figured that some of the Rocking R men had killed his old roustabout. Well, if Potter wanted to stay away, let him stay. Deputy Pete Rettiger was still at the Spur S, he related. That looked like unnecessary expense to the tax-payers, he thought; he was old enough to take care of himself without having a deputy riding herd on him.

"That deputy stays there," Judge Bates stated.

Gallatin drank again, walked outside, got on his bronc and rode out of

Singletree, cayuse on a lope. Tobacco Jones found himself wondering about the young rancher. Gallatin was smart enough — he had a good brain — but he underestimated things. He needed to mix some experience with his book-learning, and he'd be all right.

Ponce de Leon, cane extended ahead of him, crossed the room and found a chair, and Alexander sat on his lap. Tobacco Jones, suddenly disgusted for some reason, growled, "Lay off that drink, Bates, an' let's get out of here, eh?"

"You sound peeved, friend."

They went outside.

Tobacco glared at the jurist. His jaw worked with a stolid rapidity. "Bates, we've rid this range, an' got cold to our tailbones, an' what good has it done us? Nothin', that I can see."

"We know Wimberley's crooked. We know he works with Marcus and Basick."

Tobacco lifted one mittened hand. "Now, Bates, go easy. We don't know for sure. We suspects he does."

Judge Bates paid no attention. "Ponce de Leon Smith is here for a purpose. We know we've seen him out in the hills. That means he isn't blind."

"We might be wrong, Bates."

"Walt Gallatin's in danger. Marcus wants him out of the way. And I still don't think it is because of Walt's land."

"What would it be, then?"

"I got a hunch — "

"You an' your hunches. They'll put us in the poorhouse . . . or in a early grave. We know all this, then? Then why don't we act, man? Why do we sit on our tails and jump like trained seals?"

The judge allowed himself a smile. He reminded Tobacco that things would break soon. There were a few angles that would have to be clarified. This telegram would bring some response. But still Tobacco was in an argumentative mood.

"You've got some crazy telegrams

since you come here, Bates. Like this one where ol' Potter said he was headin' for some town."

"Higham," the judge supplied.

Elmer, the agent, came out of a saloon across the street, spied them, and crossed the strip. He carried a yellow envelope. "Been lookin' for you, Judge. They answered that telegram right off, it appears. Here it is. The answer you wanted from Washington, D.C."

"What does it say?"

Elmer was looking at the judge's jug. "Me. I done forgot. You read it while I take a drink . . . on you."

The judge tore it open.

16

LAWYER John Wimberley sat in his office, hands pyramided, with his elbows resting on the desk, the lamplight limning his gaunt, tall body and throwing grotesque shadows on the wall. He glanced at the clock on the file drawer across the room and scowled a little. Then he returned to inspecting his fingernails.

They were long, sloping fingernails, well kept and very clean. They were the fingernails of a man who had managed to avoid all hard physical labor. John Wimberley inspected them carefully. Then, seemingly satisfied, he gave up the minute examination. He restored his long fingers into the form of a pyramid, and let them rest in that position.

Again, he glanced at the clock.

Ten minutes later, he saw the

door-knob turn, and he heard a faint pressure put against it, heard the pressure increase until the door sagged a little. He got to his feet and said, "Step back, sir," and unbolted the lock.

Val Marcus asked, "Do you have to keep that door locked all the time?"

"I do, sir."

Marcus was in an irritable mood. The night's cold wind had brushed his gaunt, harsh jaws, making them a little red, and the wind's coldness had brought drops of water in his eyes, which he now brushed away with his dirty blue bandanna.

"I didn't want to knock, John. They might have heard it down in the saloon. You oughta move your office outa this dive and locate somewhere where a man can come in and see you without having to sneak up the back stairs." The Rocking R owner smiled a little.

"Sit down, Val."

Marcus found a chair near the stove and pulled off his sheepskin coat and mittens, draping them across the back of another chair. He warmed his hands beside the stove while Wimberley constructed his hands into another pyramid. There was a short silence, with Marcus soaking in heat, and John Wimberley thinking whatever thoughts came to his mind.

Finally Wimberley asked, "Lew Basick?"

"Higham."

Wimberley looked at his fingernails again. He found himself hoping things had gone well in Higham. The authorities would be wondering who had tipped the Higham bandits off about the gold shipment to that country seat. He remembered his confederate at the Denver mint. Val Marcus did not seem very talkative, so the lawyer let his thoughts swing south to the mint employee.

He decided, after thorough study, that his southern friend was reliable, and could be trusted to remain silent. After all, he was getting a cut back on each robbery, and this cut was many times his annual salary. Yes, he would keep what he knew to himself . . .

"And our friend, Mack Byson?"

"Higham, too."

Wimberley studied the rancher through his fingers. "You are not very talkative tonight, Val. Is there something bothering you, friend?"

Marcus studied him flatly. He looked at Wimberley's gaunt, tall frame, settled in the swivel chair, suit wrapped in folds around the bony, pointed shoulders. He looked at the bags under the sunken eyes. Then he let his gaze run to the tips of the man's fingers. This seemed to fascinate him. He looked at the well-manicured, sleek fingers. Something akin to disgust went across his face, then slowly died.

"Oh, no, nothing's bothering me! Just about now Lew's gettin' that dinero! Nothing to worry about, you say! Easy for you to say that, you tinhorn shyster, but you ain't in Lew's boots! He'll stop the slug if it comes — you won't!"

Wimberley held up his right hand for silence. His face was the same, gaunt and predatory, but his eyes, it seemed, had changed. They were flashing black beads set in black folds of thick skin.

"You raise your voice too much, Val."

Marcus settled back, watching him. He formed a hot reply, then held it. He said instead, "Blame it on the wind, John. Or blame it on Judge Bates and that shoe-string partner of his."

"Don't worry about Judge Bates, Marcus; or Tobacco Jones, either."

"They're not on this range for their health."

"Judge Bates is here to conduct a trial. Tobacco Jones is here with his friend. That is all."

"That might be what you think," Val Marcus said. "If they're here to conduct a trial, like you say, why do they ride out on open range, scouting around? Why do they scout around the Rocking R every so often?"

"You sure of that?"

"I've seen them, through glasses."

Lawyer John Wimberley played with this information. After a while he cleared his throat. "We could play this game — this same game — from some other range, Val. We don't necessarily have to have Singletree for our headquarters. If they were anybody else but Bates and Jones, I'd say kill them and give them a badland grave. But they're too wellknown, too popular, throughout the territory."

"We kill them," Marcus said, "and there'd be a dozen sheriffs and half the attorneys in the Territory camped in Singletree. They wouldn't hang us once; they'd hang us twice."

Wimberley agreed they had best keep a closer watch on Bates and Jones. He seemed disturbed by Val Marcus' information. Marcus then informed him that Mack Byson had run into the partners, too. At this, Wimberley let his eyebrows pinch down, and a scowl touched his roughly handsome features.

"And how did that happen? I thought sure that Mack would be too smart to show his face on this grass."

"He is. But he come riding along, not figuring there was a horsebacker in miles, and he rides plumb into these two, he said." Marcus stretched his legs and kicked off his overshoes. "I wonder if either of them recognized Byson? He's got quite a rep, you know."

"I doubt if they did."

"On what do you base that guess?"

"Had they recognized Byson, they'd have tried to pick him up, I figure. Or if they hadn't, Bates would have sent Rube Bennett out to do the job. No, I don't think they recognized him."

"I think along the same lines, John."

Wimberley rubbed his bloodless hands together to scrape some circulation through them. "I think we have nothing to fear from Judge Bates and his compatriot, Marcus. I am sure of that, doubly sure."

Marcus had no answer.

Some twenty minutes later, the door opened again, and this time the well foreman, Nels Tanhill, entered. Face rough from the wind, the man glanced at Wimberley, then nodded to Val Marcus, who told him to take a chair. But Tanhill did not sit down. He stood over the fire, warming his big-knuckled hands.

"Well," he said.

Wimberley looked at Marcus, smiling a little. "The man evidently wants action, Val. You or me?"

"I'll talk," Marcus said.

Tanhill listened, nodding occasionally. No, he had no objections to taking two sets of wages for one job, one set from the Rocking R and the other from young Walt Gallatin. But the Rocking R wages would have to be rather high, for he might have to cut one or two of his crew in on the deal — the driller and the winch-man. He and Val Marcus talked for some time, with Lawyer Wimberley breaking into the conversation occasionally, and

233

finally they reached terms satisfactory to both of them.

"You play square with me, Tanhill, and I'll play square with you."

"It's a deal, Marcus."

They then discussed various ways to attain their goal. Marcus stressed that he wanted the well dug properly, for when the deeds failed to come through, he himself would homestead the land now homesteaded by Walt and Sarah Gallatin. The Gallatins, although they had their original homesteads, would not have enough land and would leave Broken Creek.

Marcus stressed that, when this time came, he intended to buy out the Gallatins for a dollar and a song, and the well would then be his property.

"We'll put down a straight hole, Marcus, an' run our casin' down good. But we'll make it a slow job by deliberately jammin' casin'. There are lots of ways to slow down a well job, fella." Tanhill grinned easily. "I've done it before . . ."

Marcus asked, "All set, then?"

"I need some cash."

Marcus scowled and glanced at Wimberley, who was smiling a little. Then he pulled his gaze back to the well-digging man and asked how much advance he wanted. Tanhill named his price, and Marcus said, "I could write him a check, Wimberley."

"No check," Tanhill said.

"I ain't got that much cash on me," Marcus growled.

Wimberley went to his safe and opened it, screening the combination with his body. He counted out some gold and laid it on his desk. Tanhill moved over and counted the gold pieces, running them apart with a long forefinger. Satisfied, he pocketed them.

"Go out the back," Wimberley said. "You came in that way, too, didn't you?"

Tanhill said, "I've got some brains, lawyer."

The well-digger went out. Marcus

listened to his overshoes to go down the hall but he did not hear them. He tiptoed to the door and opened it, but the hall was empty. He shut the door, bolted it, and said, "For his size, he's light on his boots, John."

"He's tough, Val."

Marcus smiled. "He'd best play straight with Val Marcus, Wimberley, or they'll find him scattered around the hills."

Marcus left the lawyer, went down the hall and found the back stairway, and descended into the alley. He went between the Broken Latigo and Walker's Store and reached Singletree's main street.

Here and there, in various buildings, were the dim lights of kerosene lamps, showing through windows. Marcus gave the street a slow, penetrating glance, then walked out openly on the sidewalk.

He kept remembering Higham. He kept thinking of Lew Basick and Mack Byson. He steeled himself. He watched three men leave the Broken Latigo Saloon. They came out on the sidewalk, braced themselves into the wind, and came toward him. He recognized them as Judge Bates and Tobacco Jones and the blind man, Ponce de Leon. Alexander sat on Judge Bates' shoulder. Even the monkey had his head down as he faced the wind.

Ponce de Leon Smith had one hand on Tobacco's arm, the other on Judge Bates' coatsleeve. The trio and the monkey turned into the hotel. Marcus glanced at Maggie Shaw's printing shop across the street. There was a light there, and he could see the woman working on a high bench, evidently setting type. Her back was toward him, and her head bent down as she worked.

The sight of Maggie Shaw made him remember the editorial she had written, in which he had, unwittingly, been the main character. When he had read it, he had become angry, but then logic had uprooted hot temper.

She was, unknowingly, doing him a favor. She was helping him keep this range in an uproar. With trouble at home, how could local people pay any attention to trouble across the mountains?

Things were going his way. With Nels Tanhill working for him, the well-digging would be held up; with Wimberley holding those deeds in his safe, the homestead entries would be tied up.

What if Judge Bates or Walt Gallatin wired Washington about the deeds and he found out they had been mailed to Wimberley? Wimberley, of course, would claim he'd never received them; letters and wires would go back and forth, back and forth, and soon the three months would be gone. Every way, he had Walt Gallatin whipped. When this was over — and the trial completed — Walt Gallatin, by all odds, should be in the pen for murdering Joe Othon.

For the thousandth time, Val Marcus

tried to find a flaw in his scheme; again, he found none. Thus satisfied, he got his bronc and rode home, the wind behind him and sharp with fall coldness.

17

THEY opened the door with a crowbar.

They used a crowbar because they did not have a key that would fit the lock. They worked in lantern-light. The yellow light made shadows dance across the walls; it made a man's figure look out of proportion, there in the night. It flashed off the steel-blue crowbar.

They worked carefully, taking their time. It was chilly in the hall, very chilly, for morning was only four or five hours away. And the chill of the night hung to the building.

They worked carefully so that nobody could see the marks left by the crowbar, and thereby nobody would ever know how the door had been jammed. They put felt under the crowbar, doubling the felt and placing it between steel and wood, and slowly but surely, they took loose the strip in the door-jamb. They lifted this narrow strip just a little. They lifted it enough so one of them could get his jackknife under it and work the blade — the slender steel blade — against the spring-latch of the lock inside.

"That's far enough, Bates."

Judge Bates relaxed his hold on the crowbar. He watched the long fingers of Tobacco Jones, working with the pocketknife, and he rubbed his hand with his jug, using the bottom of the crockery to scratch an itchy place on his hairy hand. He watched and heard the snap of the spring-lock.

"You slid it back, partner."

Tobacco nodded. "Yeah, but it pushed back again; it's got a strong spring, Bates." He straightened suddenly. "What was that?"

Downstairs a hand had evidently turned the door-knob and turned it hard. They heard a sudden weight move against it. They listened, then heard overshoes walk away, out on the sidewalk.

"The town watchman, I guess," Judge Bates said. He shivered a little. "Open that danged door, partner."

"I'm doin' my best, Bates."

To the jurist it seemed an immeasurable time until the door swung in. Before them loomed the blackness of the room. They went inside, closing the door behind them; they went into a room that stank of stale tobacco smoke, but that still had a little heat from the pot-bellied stove. The lantern-light picked out indistinct objects, chased shadows from them, and registered their true contours. There was a desk, some chairs, the stove — and a safe, by the wall.

"Bet they're in that safe," Tobacco grunted.

Judge Bates said, "Always looking for the worst, huh, Tobacco?" He set his jug and the lantern on the desk. Downstairs, a rat scurried across the floor of the Broken Latigo Saloon. His paws made a dry, light sound, marked by great speed. "Cat must've been chasing him."

Tobacco looked up from a desk drawer. "What did you say, Bates?"

"Nothing."

"Then keep your mouth shut!"

Judge Bates drank. "You are in a sour mood, my friend. This night work doesn't sit well with you, I judge."

Tobacco looked hard at a document, holding it up to the lantern for closer scrutiny. Finally he handed the folded paper to Judge Bates. "I don't know what that is."

"A document of mechanic's lien," the jurist explained. He glanced through it. "Nothing that concerns us."

Thereafter Judge Bates rummaged through Lawyer John Wimberley's desk. And while he looked over document after document, Tobacco Jones, gaunt face dull in the lamplight, looked over the jurist's wide shoulder. Judge Bates searched every drawer in the desk, but he did not find the documents he sought.

"That's odd," he murmured.

"I tell you, they're in the safe, Bates."

The jurist straightened, rubbed his bare hands together. "Cold in here, friend. Yes, they must be in the safe."

"Maybe he didn't get them, at that."

"He got them, Tobacco. That telegram from Washington, D.C., said they had been mailed to him months ago. He's holding them up, that's what. He's playing with Marcus, like we figured for some time."

Tobacco kept looking at the safe. Finally he asked, "How could we open it? What do you know about bustin' open a safe?"

"Nothing, friend."

Tobacco scowled and chewed thoughtfully. "You must know somethin', Bates. You've seen safes that's been busted into, ain't you? Hades, I know you have! How was them safes opened?"

"Dynamite."

"We ain't got none. And if we did have some, we wouldn't know how to use it. We'd blow both us an' the safe to the promised spot." He blew hard over his shoulder, cheeks puffed. "Angel of Death, retreat!"

"One was opened with a chisel."

"How?"

Judge Bates explained that the lock had been chiseled out with a cold-chisel. The chisel had been jammed underneath and then the lock had been sprung off, the safe opened.

"But we can't work on it here, Bates. We'll wake up the whole town." Tobacco studied the safe, mentally judging its weight. "Could the two of us carry that?"

Judge Bates pushed against the top rim of the safe, tipping it a little. "Two of us could carry it." He looked at a raw-hide riata hanging on the wall. "We could make a two-man sling under it."

"I don't follow you, Bates."

The judge got the lasso, tied it the right length, secured it in loops around the four small legs, leaving two loops for them to lift by, one on each side of the safe. They both lifted, and the safe rose. Then they put it down again when Tobacco asked, "Where do we take the thing?"

The jurist ran over a number of possible places in his mind, and discarded each one. If they opened the safe in Maggie Shaw's office — No, they couldn't involve her; neither, for that matter, could they take it to their hotel room. They'd never get it upstairs without somebody catching them.

"Take it down by the creek."

"Where'll we get a chisel and hammer?"

The judge had a sudden recollection. The hostler in the livery-barn had a boxful of tools in his office. He remembered seeing some chisels and hammers there; yes, there had even been a small sledge. And the livery-barn was open all night. They took the safe out in the hall, and Tobacco mumbled, "Hope that night watchman doesn't catch us."

"You think of pleasant things."

The judge grunted, put his strength against the rope, and they carried the safe down the back stairs, the door of which the crowbar had also jimmied open. They reached the alley.

"Dark night," Tobacco said quietly.

They both caught their wind and started again. The one sticky moment came when they had to carry the safe across main street. But they cleared the strip — it seemed a hundred miles wide to the judge — and they reached the willows along the creek. The judge had carried the extinguished lantern, the wire handle hooked through the belt of his coat.

"I'll raid the livery-barn," Tobacco said.

By the time the postmaster arrived back, the jurist had the lantern lit, and had turned the safe over on its back. Tobacco had a hammer, a small sledge,

247

and four cold-chisels, all of various thickness and widths. "Nobody at the barn. The hostler must've gone home. But he left it open so's anybody could rack their broncs there."

"See the watchman?"

"Nope."

The judge got a long, slim chisel under the lock. He gave it a sharp tap with the hammer. The lock shuddered, clicked, and the judge, taking hold of the dial, lifted the door open.

"Whisky bottles!" Tobacco stared. "Just one tap, an' it opened! Oh, why, oh, why, did we lug it down here, Bates, when we could have opened it in the office? My back aches."

Judge Bates smiled grimly. "How were we to know it would open so easily? What a safe, eh?" He chuckled.

"Pot metal and bailin' wire." Tobacco held the lantern close to the dark mouth of the small safe, driving the shadows back. "Now what do you see, Bates?"

The judge took out a small buckskin

sack and shook it. "Sounds like coins." He restored the sack to its original position. He opened a small slide-drawer and found legal documents there. He took out a few of them and handed them to his partner. "There are the deeds, sir."

Tobacco cursed John Wimberley. He put the deeds in his inside coat pocket to be sure he wouldn't lose them. The judge carefully looked through the rest of the safe's contents, found nothing of any value to him, and slammed the door shut. The lock clicked, and the door would not open again.

They held the lantern close to the lock, but the edge of the dial hid the mark left by the chisel. To the casual eye, the safe had apparently not been jammed open.

"What do we do now, Bates? Heave it in the crick?"

The jurist shook his head. They would take the safe back to Lawyer Wimberley's office, he stated. At this, Tobacco Jones winced, feeling already the hard drag of carrying the safe back up the stairs. Why take it back?

"We do not want to arouse Wimberley's suspicions, Tobacco. I still think there is something bigger behind all this. If he finds his safe gone, he'll be afraid, of course; he'll pull in his horns and maybe jump the country. But if we take the safe back, safe and sound, he will probably have no suspicions. In fact, it might be a week or so until he opens it again, and it might be days until he checks to see if the deeds are in the right place."

"That's right."

They got the safe back in the sling again and started back for Wimberley's office. The watchman came down the main street, trying the doors, and passed not more than thirty feet away, entirely missing the partners who were hiding, with the safe, between two buildings. But the watchman's dog, a ratty cur, must have caught their scent, for he stopped and growled, hair upright on his skinny neck.

Tobacco mumbled, "Danged cur."

The judge put his mitten over his partner's mouth, watching the cur. The watchman said, "Come on, Rip," but the dog did not move. Finally the watchman said sternly, "Come on, you mutt! You ain't fightin' with that old tomcat tonight! Come on!"

Rip growled, trotted out of sight. Tobacco stayed with the safe, and the jurist inched ahead and watched the watchman. Finally he came back with, "Coast clear," and they hurried across the street, straining against the ropes. They went between two more buildings and reached the back stairs of the Broken Latigo Saloon.

"Close shave," Tobacco murmured. "I danged near swallered my chaw, Bates. You still hangin' onto your jug?"

"Foolish question, man."

They tugged the safe up the steps, got the back door open, carried it down the cold hall into Lawyer Wimberley's office, and restored it to its resting place. They then went outside and, with the hammer, tapped the strip down, making the door jamb look natural. Tobacco inspected the job with the lantern.

"Nobody could ever tell that jamb had been jimmied, Bates. We got the lantern and crowbar?"

The judge assured him he had their tools. Again they went out the back door, repairing it behind them, too; they went into the alley. A few minutes later, the deeds secure in Tobacco Jones' coat pocket, they entered the lobby of the hotel, where the night clerk slept, slumped deep into a chair. He did not awaken and they had no reason to wake him up.

18

WALT GALLATIN was not too happy. "I was just up to Wimberley's office, Judge, asking about those deeds. They aren't in yet. I wonder where they can be?"

"Better contact Washington, Walt."

Gallatin lit a cigarette. "Wimberley's done that. He showed me the last letter he'd received. The deeds would be along soon, that letter said. But they didn't show up."

"They'll come in."

"I sure hope so. I'd hate to lose them homesteads. I understand Marcus has already filed papers on them, figuring my deeds won't come through. I sort of wish I hadn't started to dig this well. If I lose those other homesteads, my present location's no good, not without more range."

The judge looked up from a legal

document. He assured the young rancher the deeds should be in soon, and returned his gaze to the document, in which he had no interest. He wanted Gallatin to go; he wanted to be alone.

"Well, gotta be hitting for home, Judge."

"Good luck, Walt."

Tobacco Jones came in, mentioned he had met Walt Gallatin in the corridor, and the judge put down the paper. "Old Potter," the jurist murmured, "is plumb crazy. I got this telegram this morning. Came in last night, Elmer said."

Tobacco read aloud:

"Judge, Tobacco:
Me, I've seen Higham. See you soon,
very soon.

Jim Potter."

He tossed the telegram on the jurist's desk. "That man is loco, for sure. But why does he wire us, and not Gallatin? He worked for Gallatin, not us. I hardly knew him."

"He's got some reason."

Tobacco peeled tinfoil off a fresh plug. "What would the reason be, Bates? Just what are you talkin' about?"

"I don't know, for sure."

Tobacco bit. "I sure figure you don't. For once, you spoke honest, Bates. But it's beyond yours truly."

Sheriff Rube Bennett came in, carrying the morning mail. His long, homely face looked tired, and his eyes were watery. "This job has got me down, men. Last night that crazy night watchman woke me up about four. Said he was sure somebody was down along the crick, raising ned. I went with him, but we found nobody. I asked, 'Why would anybody be down here, on a cold night like this?' an' he says, 'I heered somebody hittin' somethin' down here,' and I says, 'That was two fish fistfigtin'.'"

The judge nodded, and Tobacco chewed. "That was a good answer," the jurist praised. "You look tired, Mr. Bennett."

"I am tired."

The sheriff dumped the judge's mail out in the desk and went down to his office, boots shuffling on the floor. The judge leaned back, boots on his desk, and felt the good warmth of the stove on his back. "That watchman wasn't so dumb, at that," he remarked.

"He came too late, eh?"

"Too late."

The judge closed his eyes, for he was sleepy. He wasn't used to night work. Tobacco walked over and sorted through the mail. He remarked that Sheriff Bennett had left one of his letters here — a registered bit of mail, he noticed. Came from Higham, too.

Judge Bates opened one eye. "Higham?"

"Old Potter's town," Tobacco said, smiling.

"You got one, too, Bates." Tobacco's grimy fingers turned the letter over. "Special delivery, too. Registered. Postmaster should've delivered it hisself, but I reckon he's just too lazy."

"From Higham?"

"Yeah, from there."

"Open it."

Tobacco inserted the copper letter-opener and pulled out the contents, a thin sheet of paper. He handed it to the judge with, "You read it. Some of those words are too long."

The judge read:

"Dear Judge:
Bandits held up Higham courthouse this evening. Killed county treasurer, stole $30,000.00. Payroll for county."

"Thirty thousand, Bates!"

Judge Bates read on:

"Bandit killed, recognized as outlaw Mack Byson. Others, two in number, escaped. Believe headed north for Montana Territory. All lawmen alerted in Wyoming Territory pursuant Governor's recent edict.

Sheriff Matt Winters,
Higham, Wyoming."

Tobacco stared. "Byson — killed?"

"That's what it reads here, Tobacco."

Tobacco Jones was on his feet. "But, Bates — Hades, we saw Byson, didn't we? And he rode into the Rockin' R, didn't he?"

Judge Bates, without a moment's hesitation, ripped open Sheriff Bennett's letter, and read it, finding it identical with the one he had received. He shoved them both into a drawer as boots sounded, coming from Sheriff Bennett's office.

"Judge, I had a registered letter in my mail, an' I can't find it now. Did I leave it in here?"

"Haven't looked at my mail yet."

While Bennett watched, Judge Bates skimmed through his mail, then shook his head. "It isn't here. Are you sure you had the letter?"

"Sure looked like one. Besides, I signed for it."

"You had a package, too." Tobacco Jones reminded him. "Maybe you had to sign for that. Was it insured?"

Sheriff Bennett scowled, trying to remember. "I'm so danged sleepy my memory's left me. I guess it was that package I signed for." He shuffled out and went into his office, the partners hearing the door close behind him.

"Close the door, Jones!"

Tobacco closed the door. He stood, back against the panel, chewing, thinking. Judge Bates' boots were now on the floor. The jurist sat and looked down at his jug, then methodically reached for it and uncorked it. But he did not drink right away. He played with the cork.

"What do you say, partner?"

Tobacco spoke slowly. "Byson was killed in Higham. We know that. We figure that was Byson we trailed, that rode into Marcus' Rocking R. We're sure he was Byson, ain't we?"

Judge Bates nodded.

"Then Potter, he wires from Higham. That ties in there somewhere. The whole thing centers around Higham, I'd say. Ain't that right, Bates?"

The jurist nodded again.

Tobacco waited. "Well?"

"How else do you see it?"

Tobacco considered, never missing a stroke with his jaws. "Well, you don't want Sheriff Bennett in on this, whatever it is, or turns out to be."

"He'd gum things up. Any more?"

"That's all, Bates. Now you?"

The judge reminded that Mack Byson, now dead, had ridden into Val Marcus' Rocking R; that tied Byson and Marcus together, didn't it? That tied Marcus into the Higham robbery.

Tobacco shook his head. "But Marcus has been in town the last few days; he was in last night. He wasn't in Higham. He couldn't have been."

"Basick? Did you see him?"

Tobacco rubbed his jaw thoughtfully. "No," he admitted, "I ain't seen Lew Basick for some days now." He studied his partner through his lifeless eyes. "But, Lem, you're imaginin' a heap."

"Not imagination, friend; facts, tied together. Ponce de Leon Smith is on this range for another reason than to peddle pencils and tinware and torture people on that violin. He can't play it worth a damn."

"What about that?"

"I'll bet he never had a fiddle in his hands before he came here. I'll lay odds on that."

"But's he's blind," Tobacco said.

Judge Bates tried a new angle. "Byson rode to see Marcus, and Marcus and John Wimberley are good friends. That brings this down to Wimberley, doesn't it? And Wimberley pretends to be Gallatin's friend."

"Still guessin', Bates."

Judge Bates bit his bottom lip. "This won't be guess work long," he said shortly.

"Lead the way, Bates."

The jurist was checking his .45. Satisfied, he returned the pistol to leather, got his Winchester .30-30 from the corner, verified its loads, saw that extra brass cartridges rode in the magazine. He asked, "My shotgun is on my saddle, isn't it?"

"She be there, Bates."

Judge Bates stood looking at the rifle. "We need some chuck. We can get that at Gallatin's. No, we better pick it up in town. Walt might wonder what was going on, and get suspicious."

"I'm suspicious," Tobacco said, grinning.

"You know darn well what's ahead." The judge's eyes were serious. "We head out and watch the Rocking R. Me, I figure it's a roosting place for buzzards; them buzzards will come home to roost right pronto, I figure."

Already Tobacco was cramming cartridges into his cartridge belt. He jacked his rifle open with, "They might, at that, Bates." He snapped the breech shut. "We need some .30-30 shells an' some shotgun cartridges. Wonder if a man can buy ten-gauge shotgun shells in this burg? They're an off size and hard to get."

"I got an unopened package on my saddle."

They went to the Mercantile, where they bought some supplies — cans of beans, some coffee, some salt, a slab of bacon. Tobacco picked up a tin can as they walked down the alley. "Make a good cofee pot, Bates."

"There's Ponce de Leon Smith."

The blind peddler had come out of the depot. For once, Alexander wasn't with him, and when Judge Bates inquired about the animal, Ponce de Leon said the monkey had a touch of cold, and he was keeping him in for the day. He mentioned he would be in the hotel lobby that afternoon and they would start a whist game. The judge told him they would be out at the Gallatin Ranch for a few days.

Ponce de Leon Smith nodded, then continued on toward the hotel. At the livery-barn, Tobacco said, "What was that bum doing in the depot?"

"He'd received a telegram. Didn't you see the edge of the envelope sticking out of his pocket?"

"Now who'd wire to him?"

"Maybe he's got a woman friend somewhere, a second Maggie Shaw."

Tobacco smiled. "If he has, heaven help him."

19

THE stove was warm, and outside the wind blew strong. The wind lifted the loose snow and built it into drifts. The snow piled against sagebrush and greasewood and built into banks of whiteness. But inside, it was warm. For the lignite in the stove blazed and released its heat.

Lawyer John Wimberley paid no attention to the heat. The moment before, he had been comfortable, dozing in his swivel chair, listening to the cold wind in the eaves, thinking how warm it was in his office. He had remembered he had a mechanic's lien to file with the recorder before the day ended, for this was the last day the lien could be filed. The local carpenter had built a room onto the barber's house. The barber had held back payment. Therefore the carpenter had been forced to put a lien on the barber's property. These were all small items but, if they were added all together, they made a nice income for John Wimberley.

Accordingly, Wimberley had gone to his safe to get the paper. He'd go down into the Broken Latigo and get Old Si Clemons to take it to the courthouse. Old Si would do it for a drink. The lock on the safe had, for some reason, worked stiffly, much more stiffly than usual. Maybe it needed oil, the lawyer thought. Some day he'd oil it again.

He found the mechanic's lien, which was on top of Walt Gallatin's deeds, and he decided to check the expiration date on the deeds again. But the deeds were gone!

At first he couldn't believe it; he had merely placed them in a different section of the safe. But after searching the safe, he still found no deeds; panic and alarm touched him, but he managed to push them aside.

Maybe he had put the deeds in his desk?

Thereupon he had searched his desk. The longer he looked, the more panicky he got — he couldn't help it. When he had finished, his bony hands were trembling. He stood silent and straight and considered.

He stood there for a few minutes, and then he went to work. He went through every paper or document he had. What he thought dangerous, he threw into the stove. He had a grim thought. He was an ambassador, ready to leave a country, and he was burning his legal papers. Sure, he was an ambassador. An ambassador of tough luck for Broken Creek and Singletree . . .

He left his safe open, got his rifle from the corner, and walked into the Broken Latigo, dressed for the trail — overshoes over his polished riding-boots, thick California pants, heavy underwear and woollen shirt, short-coat under his long sheepskin. He ordered a drink.

Smokey said, "You going out coyote hunting, Wimberley?"

"Wolf hunting." A ghost of a smile.

Smokey did not notice the smile. "Won't find many wolves around here. Most of them have been killed off. Heaps of coyotes, though. Hides are worth a little bit now, with cold weather making them prime."

Wimberley downed his whisky. He bought a quart of Old Rome and crammed it in his coat pocket. His elbows on the bar, he looked over the Broken Latigo, his look slow and probing.

"Seen Judge Bates and Jones lately, Smokey?"

Smokey told him that according to gossip, the judge and postmaster had gone out to Walt Gallatin's for an extended visit prior to the opening of court term. Wimberley nodded and went outside. He got his horse at the livery. He saddled him.

"Ain't takin' your buggy?" the hostler asked.

Wimberley glanced at the ornate affair. He sent a glance at his team, munching hay in a stall. "You can have that buggy and that team."

The hostler thought he was joking. "Oh, sure, Wimberley, sure. I know how much you paid for that team and buggy."

Wimberley lifted himself into saddle, settled down between fork and cantle. He rode out at a trot, the wind behind him. The sun was hidden behind boiling storm-clouds that swept down from the Rockies.

When he rode into the yard at the Spur S, Walt Gallatin was hauling hay from a stack down on the creek bottom, putting it on another stack beside his barn. He leaned on his pitchfork, face ruddy from his work and the wind, and allowed it looked like a right smart winter was ahead.

Wimberley nodded, looking at the house. Gallatin slapped his pitchfork into the load, tied the reins around a wagonwheel, and they went to the house. Sarah was sewing and Mattie was cutting up a mail-order catalogue, making dolls out of it. They had a drink from Wimberley's bottle.

"Good liquor," Walt said.

"Judge Bates carries good whisky, I understand."

Walt said, "That's true." He went on to say he hadn't seen Judge Bates for some days now; he'd expected the judge and Tobacco to ride out, too. Wimberley nodded, said they probably didn't want to ride such a distance in such rough weather. He had learned what he wanted.

"Anything new on those deeds, John?"

Sarah stopped sewing, looking at him. Wimberley told them the deeds would be in inside of two days, according to the last Washington reports. He said goodbye and got his horse and rode toward Singletree. But, once out of sight, he swung off the trail and headed for the Rocking R.

He rode fast. Snow was dropping, swirling around his gaunt form as he leaned against the storm, mittens

270

braced on his saddle's fork. He was glad it was snowing. Nobody would then see him ride to Marcus' ranch.

A guard challenged him when he rode into the Rocking R. The lawyer drew in and said, "Blacky, eh? When did you get in?"

"Yesterday mornin'."

"Where's Lew Basick?"

Blacky shrugged. "We split up, right out of Higham. We divided the loot as fast as we could and split trails. I went one way, Lew one, an' Jackass went his way. Jackass near didn't make it to Higham. He got drunk an' got in jail at Twin Buttes, but he busted out in time to get in on the robbery."

Wimberley looked up the peak of a mountain, almost hidden by snow. "Seems odd Lew isn't in yet. Jackass get in?"

"Neither of them."

The roustabout took the attorney's bronc into the barn. Blacky and Wimberley went to the house, where Val Marcus was standing with his back to the fireplace, watching them enter. The Rocking R owner was scowling.

"Long ride in such cold weather, John." Marcus was sarcastic. "You afraid we wouldn't cut you in?"

Wimberley said, "Somebody stole those deeds, Val"

Val Marcus studied him. Then he smiled and said, "Poor joke, John. Poor joke."

"No joke, damn it!"

Marcus asked, "Explain yourself."

John Wimberley told about looking for the Gallatin deeds, not finding them.

"Who do you reckon did it, John?" Marcus spoke hoarsely.

"I figure Bates and Jones."

Marcus considered. "Maybe Gallatin got suspicious of you and made the robbery. That's possible."

"But not probable." The lawyer told about his talk with Walt Gallatin and that Gallatin had asked about the deeds. "Gallatin has a tough temper. There's nothing slick about him. If he'd got those deeds, he'd've jumped me pronto."

"That's right," Blacky said.

Marcus glanced at his rider. "Where are Bates and Jones now, Wimberley?"

"Nobody knows."

Marcus studied him. "Explain yourself."

Wimberley told them that Jones and Bates were supposed to be at Gallatin's Spur S. But they were not there, and not in town. Their broncs were gone. "They've been gone two days, I figure."

Blacky looked at Marcus. Marcus met his gaze. Blacky murmured, "I wonder, boss; I wonder . . ."

Marcus said, "That might be why Basick and Jackass haven't ridden in yet. Bates and Jones might've jumped them out in the badlands. Have you heard Sheriff Bennett mention the Higham robbery? He must've heard about it from the capital by now."

No, Bennett had not mentioned the robbery, and that was puzzling. Bennett

273

was staying close to his stove. But why would Bates and Jones jump Basick or Jackass? Surely they had no reason to tie the Rocking R into the Higham hold-up.

Marcus growled, "There are lots of loopholes here. How straight is that gent you got in the mint in Denver? What if he started to meow? He'd talk about all of us."

Blacky said, "Let's drink and drift, boss."

Marcus stood silent. Wimberley watched him. Blacky watched him. Somewhere a clock ticked. The tick sounded loud — unnaturally loud.

"I got a lot to leave behind," Marcus finally said.

Wimberley smiled. "You might leave your life behind, if you stay here. You've been on a few of those raids, you know. You've killed two men, I think. I believe it is two. One in Snowden and the other — "

"That's enough of that, tinhorn!"

Wimberley shrugged. "Facts, friend;

facts that hold up in a court . . . if somebody decides to talk plenty."

"Basick is gone," Blacky reminded him. "He should be home by now. So should Jackass. Where are they? Has Bates got them? Makin' them talk!"

"Basick won't sing."

"No, he won't." Blacky raised one eyebrow. "But how about Jackass? You get him drunk, he blabs."

"Right," Wimberley maintained.

Boots came across the porch, and Lew Basick entered. Whiskers covered his jaw — the pale whiskers of an albino — and snow hung to his overcoat and angora chaps. His pale, thin face showed weariness.

"Jackass ain't in yet?"

Marcus shook his head.

Basick said, "Gimme a drink?" and Wimberley handed him his bottle. Basick lowered it with, "He should be here. He was ahead of me. What became of him?"

"Maybe the law got him," Blacky said.

Marcus cut in with, "Maybe Judge Bates nabbed him."

Basick studied the Rocking R boss, eyes dull over the bottle. He asked him to explain himself. Wimberley told what he knew, and Basick nodded, and then Val Marcus cut in. Basick said, "We drift, and pronto. If Jackass gets caught he'll talk — He'll talk — "

Val Marcus stood silent, looking around the big living-room. Wimberley caught the significance of the gaze.

"You don't stand to lose anything, Marcus. If this blows over, you can come back. If it doesn't, I have a few attorney friends who can handle your — shall we call it 'estate'? But we'd better all drift and wait and watch."

Marcus nodded.

20

THE old man stared at them. He wet his lips with his red tongue, and then said, "By Hades, if'n it ain't Judge Bates an' Tobaccer Jones."

"Talk," Judge Bates said.

Old Potter rubbed his whiskery jaw. "You got my telegrams, I take it. Wal, I woke up in the boxcar, savvy. Somebody slugged me at the Spur S an' loaded me in that car."

"We know that," Tobacco said.

Old Potter said, "I'm awful dry." He looked at the judge's jug, but the jurist did not offer him a drink. "Well, thet Twin Butte sheriff jailed me, as per Bates' orders. He threw me into a cell with a gent named Jackass."

"How long were his ears?" Judge Bates asked, smiling.

"Long enough. But his tongue was

longer. Thet Twin Butte sheriff didn't know I had a bottle of Old Crow on me. Jackass drunk almost the whole thing. We got friendly; we put our arms aroun' each other. We was suddenly old pals."

"Drunken louts," Tobacco grumbled.

"Clip it short," Judge Bates advised.

Old Potter did. Jackass informed him, in a lubricated moment, that he was going up north to Higham, and he hinted of great monetary reward up there. He mentioned a few names, too. They had given Potter his clue.

"I was purty well oiled myself, men, but them words whipped me plumb sober. I sure was lucky to git slugged an' land up in such company. What do you call a happenin' like that?"

"A coincidence," the judge supplied.

"That's right, a coeencedence! Well, Jackass wants me along — we busts that tin can of a jail. Peeled it off'n us with some hacksaw blades he had sewed in his boot." Here Potter shook his head and wet his lips again. "But me, I'd learned enough. I figgered that when Jackass sobered up he might remember, an' when he remembered he might get scared, an' he might shoot me for knowin' so much."

"So you jerked stakes?" Tobacco wanted to know.

Potter nodded. "I did just that, men. I watched Higham — even stole this ol' nag I'm astraddle — got him out of a sod-buster's barn — " His whiskers shook sadly. "Now I'm a thief, a wanted man."

The judge told him that they would clear his record, locating the farmer and either returning or paying for the nag. He'd clear things with the Twin Butte sheriff, too.

"And the rest of the story, Mr. Potter?"

They were sitting their bronc in a clump of young pines. The wind soughed through the trees and made old Potter's low voice hard to understand. Below them tumbled the snow drifts on the mountain's side, and beyond it were more mountains and more pine and spruce.

He'd spotted the hold-up and, true to Jackass' drunken prediction, Lew Basick was in on it, and so was Blacky. He'd cut across country ahead of them and had hoped to contact the partners in Singletree. "But meetin' you out here is better, Bates. I wonder if they are suspicious?"

"I wouldn't be a bit surprised."

They decided to watch the Rocking R men ride in, then jump them one at a time. But Blacky evidently got through their blockade at night, for the next morning they saw him on the Rocking R.

"Too big a country to watch," Potter mumbled. "Reckon they split up to throw the sheriff off their trail, an' might trek in one at a time."

"Looks that way," the judge agreed.

They got Jackass the next afternoon. He came loping down an old trail, singing a little, for the Rocking R Ranch was in sight; his long ride was over. His pony, sensing oats and hay — and a warm stall ahead, broke into a wild lope. He loped through a clump of trees. When he loped out of them, his saddle was empty. Tobacco Jones rode in and caught the horse by the bridle-reins.

Old Potter was kneeling beside Jackass. "He hit that rope with his neck, Bates, and it shut off his wind. His Adam's apple is stickin' out the back."

"He'll live, Potter."

Jackass' eyes finally opened and found Potter's homely face. "How'd I get back in jail — " He sat up and stared at them. "What happened?"

"You rode into our rope," the judge explained. "We had it tied from that tree to another one."

Jackass looked at Potter. "Who are these gents?"

Old Potter had some explaining to do. When he had finished Jackass sat up, rubbing his Adam's apple and studying the judge and postmaster.

Finally he said, "I don't know what you're talkin' about, old man."

"Take him back in the brush," Judge Bates ordered.

They had built a lean-to in the pines, slight protection against the elements. They laid Jackass on the blanket, and he tried to sit up, but Judge Bates had his thick knee on the outlaw's chest, holding him down.

"Be good, or we'll slug you to sleep."

Jackass puffed, then asked, "What'd you aim to do, Bates?"

Judge Bates did not answer. "Give me my jug, Tobacco; uncork it." He took the uncorked vessel and jammed it between Jackass' tobacco-colored teeth. Jackass had to swallow or be drowned. He swallowed.

Judge Bates pulled the jug back. Jackass coughed, spewing whisky. He wiped his hand across his mouth. "Nice medicine, Bates. But I still don't savvy what you aim to do."

The judge took his knee off the man's chest. "Take another slug."

An hour later, they had Jackass roaring drunk. He sat and sang songs, and subtly, through correct prompting, the judge got him to talking about his outlawry. The whisky made Jackass boastful.

"You talk," the judge prompted, "an I'll make it easier on you."

Jackass leered at him. "That a promise, Bates?"

The judge said it was. Tobacco said so, too. Jackass looked at Potter. "What do you say, o'l cell mate?"

"They got enough to hang you," Potter said. "The county treasurer got murdered in that Higham hold-up. Maybe you killed him, eh?"

"Me, I never gut-shot him. Lew Basick shot him; cold blood, too. He had no reason — "

The judge reminded him that Basick and Blacky — yes, and Val Marcus and John Wimberley — were doomed to hit the jail-house soon. One of them might claim he, Jackass, killed the treasurer, and he might die on the gallows for a crime he'd never committed. From his standpoint, it would appear that the man who talked first would come out the best.

"Of course, you'll have to go to jail, but turning state's evidence will cut your sentence."

"I'll talk plenty," Jackass assured them.

That night, John Wimberley rode into the Rocking R, and Judge Bates, watching from the mountainside, looked long at Tobacco Jones. "The rats are scared, my friend. A nickel to a doughnut that Wimberley has missed those deeds. We'd better watch close."

"We're outnumbered, Bates."

"Four of them, three of us." The judge counted. "Blacky, Marcus, Wimberley. And Basick. And we might intercept Basick yet."

"Not if he comes through at night. Too dark, Judge."

And Tobacco's prophecy proved correct. For two hours later the postmaster rode into the brush hiding the lean-to and said, "Basick just came in. I was watchin' the ranch-house and I saw him when the door opened. I could recognize him in the lamp-light."

The judge dismounted. "I just rode in, too, Tobacco. Came from the canyon." He uncorked his jug. "Night too dark, I guess."

Old Potter looked up from the lean-to. "What's next, Bates?"

"Ride down and get them, Potter."

They tied Jackass hand and foot. Not that it made much difference to him, for old John Barleycorn had already tied him into a deep drunken sleep. They got their broncs and rode toward the Rocking R.

"Jackass'll have a terrible hangover," Potter offered.

They drew rein in the brush and got their weapons. The judge and Tobacco took their sawed-off shotguns, and Potter had the judge's rifle, for he had not got his old gun, which the Twin Butte sheriff had taken from him. "I left in too much of a dust to collect my weapon, Bates."

They went behind the Rocking R barn. Beyond the barn were the lights of the house. Down on the flat a cow bawled, evidently standing by the barb-wire fence that separated her from a haystack.

Their plan called for them to go into the barn and lay a trap. Therefore they went ahead, leaving their broncs in the brush, and they entered the barn by the rear door. They went inside and shut the door behind them.

The mixed odors of a barn met them: the smell of manure; the dry smell of leather — saddles, bridles, harnesses; the smutty odor of hay in stalls. The place was dark and chilly.

Tobacco murmured, "What was that?"

The judge had heard it, too. A long, scraping sound, like a boot moving over a plank, somewhere ahead. They stood tense, listening. They did not hear the sound again. There was only the noise of horses chewing at hay and grain.

"Probably a rat, Tobacco."

The front door of the barn was closed. The judge found a lantern, lit it, and saw a block and tackle, hanging from a beam in the middle of the aisle. He hooked the hook around the lantern's bail and lifted it up to the beam made of hewed-out pine. The yellow rays were dim and shadowy, but they showed the barn rather clearly.

Old Potter said, "I'll take the haymow." He climbed the rickety ladder and pulled his legs out of sight in the hay-hole. They heard him move around, then become silent.

Tobacco shivered. "It's cold, Bates."

"You sure it's only the cold?"

"Bates, I'll — "

"Get in that manger, Tobacco, and good luck."

Tobacco looked at him. "Good luck to you, too, pal."

The Cowtrail postmaster dragged his long frame into the manger and settled down, hidden by the wide thick planks. The judge debated a moment, then stepped inside the room built in the corner. It was a room where sacks of feed were stored. The air was close and there was no ventilation.

He seated himself on a sack of oats, watching through the narrow slit of space he had left between the door and its frame. Through this slit he could see the barn's entire length, but anybody glancing at the door would think it only open a little, and could not see the jurist in the darkened background.

And so, stationed, they waited.

Time ran by, and the judge's muscles grew tense. He smiled, remembering how Tobacco Jones had crammed his length into the manger, and reckoned his partner's legs would really be stiff. Old Potter, up in the haymow, would have it easier — the old gent was probably asleep by now, curled up in the hay.

More time passed.

Finally, the judge came wide awake, for he had heard boots — and voices — coming toward the barn. He looked out a knothole and saw that the house was entirely dark. He heard the boots and voices come closer, but he could not make out the men in the dark.

The front door opened, and by this time the jurist was at the feed-room door, looking at the men who had entered. They were ready for the trail with blankets, canned chuck in a sack, and rifles under their arms.

Val Marcus said, "Who left this lantern on, anyway? An' who hung it up to the beam that-a-way?"

"You got me," Basick said. "It was dark when I rode in."

Blacky said, "Maybe the roustabout had some crazy idea. He gets that way at times."

"I don't savvy it," Marcus repeated.

Blacky led a sorrel out of a stall, started smoothing his saddle-blanket over the broad back. Basick was tossing his kak on a blue roan gelding. Wimberley was cinching his hull down on a black.

Marcus stood silent, looking the

barn over very carefully. Judge Bates' breath scarcely raised his thick chest. He watched, and once Marcus looked straight at the feed-room, and the jurist moved back. He half-expected Marcus to come to the door, and he waited for the man's boots.

"Get a hoss, boss," Blacky said.

Marcus said, "That lantern — I don't savvy it," and he went to a stall, where he threw his Navajo saddle-blanket on a big dun. Blacky led his sorrel out into the corridor and waited, rifle in saddle-boot. Wimberley put his rifle in its scabbard and waited beside his bronc. Basick cinched down his hull and looked at his rifle's loads.

Judge Bates noticed each man wore his short-gun strapped outside his sheepskin coat or mackinaw. He didn't like that. He waited until Val Marcus led out his bronc. Everybody had rifle in saddle-boot. They were leading their broncs toward the front door when he stepped out.

The door hinges squeaked, and they

turned and faced him, mittened hands running for their gun grips. But mittened hands stopped when they looked at the judge's shotgun.

Marcus asked, his voice shaky, "What is this, Bates?"

"Behind us," Wimberley said hurriedly. For Tobacco Jones had come up in the stall. He had hidden himself under hay, and long wisps of bluejoint hung to his shoulders. "The jig is up," he said.

Marcus moved to one side. He had slipped off his mitten and let it fall to the sod floor. Blacky quit staring, his first surprise gone. Lew Basick, too, had dropped a mitten, and Basick's eyes were darting, pale pinpoints in the yellow lamplight.

"I'm up here, too," a voice said from the haymow.

John Wimberley, his gaunt face yellow and sick, glanced up at the ladder, but Val Marcus said, "That's old Potter. I'd know that squeak anywhere."

Wimberley whipped his gaze back. He looked hard at Judge Bates. "Bates, you're holding up law-abiding citizens. You'll pay for this in court, I promise that."

"We'll get into court," the jurist promised, "but I'll be the judge and you'll be the prisoner. We got those deeds you held from Walt Gallatin. Never mind how we got them. That's a federal offense, Wimberley: tampering with government documents, and holding them."

"That's a small charge," Wimberley said unsteadily.

The jurist was watching Marcus and Basick. Both of them were looking around, looking at Tobacco, up at Potter, and the jurist knew they were weighing their chances.

"Why try to hold us?" Marcus wanted to know.

Potter's squeaky voice cut in. "I'll tell you why, you ignoramus! Jackass is back in the bresh, an' Jackass talked. You don't know it, but us two was in jail together, over in Twin Buttes. He tol' me plenty."

Basick turned his eyes on Marcus. "Jackass was in that jail, he told me." Basick was silent, his lip quivering a little.

"Basick killed the treasurer in that Higham hold-up. Jackass will swear to that. Jackass will swear to another thing, too, Marcus. You shot down Joe Othon. You hated him and sent him against Walt Gallatin. Then, in the dark, you killed Othon — shot him from his bronc — and you laid the blame on Walt Gallatin. Jackass only spent three days here, then went on because you didn't want him around — might look suspicious."

"Jackass is a liar," Marcus stated.

"I figure otherwise," Judge Bates said. "And remember, men, I'll sit on the bench, listening to your trials."

Wimberley almost screamed, "With him on the bench, we'll all go to jail, or hang."

Basick had his pistol out. He shot

once, aiming at Tobacco, who went down in the stall. Tobacco's shotgun boomed, but the judge figured it shot its pellets into the ceiling.

Marcus howled, "Get them!"

Old Potter's rifle sent Lew Basick to his knees. Basick dropped his Colt and tried to grab it, but he fell down on his face. Marcus grabbed his gun, shot at Judge Bates, but in his haste, he shot wide. And the judge shot wide, too.

Wimberley was hollering, begging in a high-pitched voice that they spare him. Horses reared and pawed, then bolted down the aisle. They smashed into the closed door and ripped it from its hinges and disappeared into the night.

Old Potter launched his skinny frame from the haymow, knocking Blacky to his knees just as the gunman fired. The force sent Blacky's bullet into the ground. Old Potter, wild from his lunge, rolled off Blacky; by this time, Tobacco Jones was out of the manger. The postmaster brought his rifle down, and Blacky forgot his gun.

A horse had shielded Marcus, who grabbed for his stirrup, and missed. Before the judge could fire again, Marcus was running out the door, gun talking. He shot twice, hitting a horse once, and then disappeared out the front door.

"Get him!" Tobacco hollered.

Wimberley was still hollering, begging for mercy. Blacky was still sleeping. Basick lay very still. Old Potter, getting up from his dive, held an arm that plainly was broken. Tobacco started out the front door, limping terribly.

"Sprained my ankle — fell in the manger — "

Judge Bates grabbed his partner. "Don't go out the front — you'll be limned in the light — out the back."

"I'll watch these gents," Potter hollered.

The judge, followed by the limping Tobacco, ran down the manure-littered aisle, and out the smashed rear door. They hurried along the building, figuring

Marcus would run to the house and hole up.

"That bronc — he got in the way!" The judge was panting. "Otherwise I'd've downed Marcus!"

"Lissen, Bates!"

They stopped, for ahead, up by the house, rifle-fire had sounded, mixed with six-gun reports. The sounds died as suddenly as had begun.

"Who was that, Bates?"

"One must've been Val Marcus, I'd say. He had a six-shooter. But the other — I don't know." The judge cupped his hands around his mouth. "Who's there? This is Judge Lemanuel Bates."

"Me," a voice called. "Your friend, Bates."

Judge Bates scowled, catching his wind. The voice sounded mighty familiar. Tobacco said, "I know that voice."

"Who's *me*?" the judge hollered.

The lantern light, pushing through the open front door of the barn, showed a thin man approaching, carrying a rifle. Tobacco stared, fingers digging into Judge Bates sheepskin.

"That's — Bates, are my eyes right?"

"They're right!"

Ponce de Leon Smith had shed his ornate suit with its faded braids. Gone too were his dark glasses. "I hated to kill Marcus, but he forced me to, Judge Bates. What are you men doing here?"

The judge told him.

"I always claimed this gent wasn't blind," Tobacco stated.

Ponce de Leon Smith, whose real name turned out to be Bill Beggins, was a federal agent, and he had trailed Marcus and Wimberley for some time. He had come into Singletree disguised as a blind violinist.

"'Fraid they might suspect me, Bates."

The judge had had enough for one night. He said, "Where's my jug?" and Tobacco, who had also had enough, found it in the barn. Bill Beggins said he would take charge here, so the partners rode toward Singletree.

The wind had stopped, for once; the moon was rising. The judge took a drink, and sighed. Tobacco looked at him and said, "Well, no trial for Walt Gallatin now, Bates."

"No trial."

"We'll be ridin' home in a day or so, I reckon." Tobacco Jones spat and scowled. "Or will we have to wait for the trial of Blacky an' Wimberley an' Jackass?"

"I'll try them in the morning, Tobacco." The judge was silent. "It'll be a speedy trial. Very speedy . . . and adequate."

"Then tomorrow afternoon we'll be headin' for Cowtrail?"

"Headin' home." The judge looked at his partner's homely face, barely discernible in the moonlight. "You'll break Maggie Shaw's heart."

"Let it bust, Bates!"

BOOTHILL RIDERS
RIDERS OF DEATH
BONANZA AT WISHBONE
TWO GUNS NORTH
THE RAWHIDE MEN
WYOMING SHOWDOWN
FRONTIER LAWMAN
THE TALL TEXAN
COWTHIEF CLANTON
WEST OF BARBWIRE
BUCKSKIN CHALLENGE
COYOTES OF WILLOW BROOK
FIGHTING RAMROD

Other titles in the Linford Western Library:

TOP HAND
Wade Everett

The Broken T was big. But no ranch is big enough to let a man hide from himself.

GUN WOLVES OF LOBO BASIN
Lee Floren

The Feud was a blood debt. When Smoke Talbot found the outlaws who gunned down his folks he aimed to nail their hide to the barn door.

SHOTGUN SHARKEY
Marshall Grover

The westbound coach carrying the indomitable Larry and Stretch headed for a shooting showdown.

FIGHTING RAMROD
Charles N. Heckelmann

Most men would have cut their losses, but Frazer counted the bullets in his guns and said he'd soak the range in blood before he'd give up another inch of what was his.

LONE GUN
Eric Allen

Smoke Blackbird had been away too long. The Lequires had seized the Blackbird farm, forcing the Indians and settlers off, and no one seemed willing to fight! He had to fight alone.

THE THIRD RIDER
Barry Cord

Mel Rawlins wasn't going to let anything stand in his way. His father was murdered, his two brothers gone. Now Mel rode for vengeance.

ARIZONA DRIFTERS
W. C. Tuttle

When drifting Dutton and Lonnie Steelman decide to become partners they find that they have a common enemy in the formidable Thurston brothers.

TOMBSTONE
Matt Braun

Wells Fargo paid Luke Starbuck to outgun the silver-thieving stagecoach gang at Tombstone. Before long Luke can see the only thing bearing fruit in this eldorado will be the gallows tree.

HIGH BORDER RIDERS
Lee Floren

Buckshot McKee and Tortilla Joe cut the trail of a border tough who was running Mexican beef into Texas. They stopped the smuggler in his tracks.

BRETT RANDALL, GAMBLER
E. B. Mann

Larry Day had the choice of running away from the law or of assuming a dead man's place. No matter what he decided he was bound to end up dead.

THE GUNSHARP
William R. Cox

The Eggerleys weren't very smart. They trained their sights on Will Carney and Arizona's biggest blood bath began.

THE DEPUTY OF SAN RIANO
Lawrence A. Keating and
Al. P. Nelson

When a man fell dead from his horse, Ed Grant was spotted riding away from the scene. The deputy sheriff rode out after him and came up against everything from gunfire to dynamite.

FARGO: MASSACRE RIVER
John Benteen

The ambushers up ahead had now blocked the road. Fargo's convoy was a jumble, a perfect target for the insurgents' weapons!

SUNDANCE: DEATH IN THE LAVA
John Benteen

The Modoc's captured the wagon train and its cargo of gold. But now the halfbreed they called Sundance was going after it . . .

HARSH RECKONING
Phil Ketchum

Five years of keeping himself alive in a brutal prison had made Brand tough and careless about who he gunned down . . .

FARGO: PANAMA GOLD
John Benteen

With foreign money behind him, Buckner was going to destroy the Panama Canal before it could be completed. Fargo's job was to stop Buckner.

FARGO: THE SHARPSHOOTERS
John Benteen

The Canfield clan, thirty strong were raising hell in Texas. Fargo was tough enough to hold his own against the whole clan.

PISTOL LAW
Paul Evan Lehman

Lance Jones came back to Mustang for just one thing — revenge! Revenge on the people who had him thrown in jail.

HELL RIDERS
Steve Mensing

Wade Walker's kid brother, Duane, was locked up in the Silver City jail facing a rope at dawn. Wade was a ruthless outlaw, but he was smart, and he had vowed to have his brother out of jail before morning!

DESERT OF THE DAMNED
Nelson Nye

The law was after him for the murder of a marshal — a murder he didn't commit. Breen was after him for revenge — and Breen wouldn't stop at anything . . . blackmail, a frameup . . . or murder.

DAY OF THE COMANCHEROS
Steven C. Lawrence

Their very name struck terror into men's hearts — the Comancheros, a savage army of cutthroats who swept across Texas, leaving behind a bloodstained trail of robbery and murder.

SUNDANCE: SILENT ENEMY
John Benteen

A lone crazed Cheyenne was on a personal war path. They needed to pit one man against one crazed Indian. That man was Sundance.

LASSITER
Jack Slade

Lassiter wasn't the kind of man to listen to reason. Cross him once and he'll hold a grudge for years to come — if he let you live that long.

LAST STAGE TO GOMORRAH
Barry Cord

Jeff Carter, tough ex-riverboat gambler, now had himself a horse ranch that kept him free from gunfights and card games. Until Sturvesant of Wells Fargo showed up.

McALLISTER
ON THE
COMANCHE CROSSING
Matt Chisholm

The Comanche, McAllister owes them a life — and the trail is soaked with the blood of the men who had tried to outrun them before.

QUICK-TRIGGER COUNTRY
Clem Colt

Turkey Red hooked up with Curly Bill Graham's outlaw crew. But wholesale murder was out of Turk's line, so when range war flared he bucked the whole border gang alone . . .

CAMPAIGNING
Jim Miller

Ambushed on the Santa Fe trail, Sean Callahan is saved by two Indian strangers. But there'll be more lead and arrows flying before the band join Kit Carson against the Comanches.

GUNSLINGER'S RANGE
Jackson Cole

Three escaped convicts are out for revenge. They won't rest until they put a bullet through the head of the dirty snake who locked them behind bars.

RUSTLER'S TRAIL
Lee Floren

Jim Carlin knew he would have to stand up and fight because he had staked his claim right in the middle of Big Ike Outland's best grass.

THE TRUTH ABOUT SNAKE RIDGE
Marshall Grover

The troubleshooters came to San Cristobal to help the needy. For Larry and Stretch the turmoil began with a brawl and then an ambush.

WOLF DOG RANGE
Lee Floren

Will Ardery would stop at nothing, unless something stopped him first — like a bullet from Pete Manly's gun.

DEVIL'S DINERO
Marshall Grover

Plagued by remorse, a rich old reprobate hired the Texas Trouble-shooters to deliver a fortune in greenbacks to each of his victims.

GUNS OF FURY
Ernest Haycox

Dane Starr, alias Dan Smith, wanted to close the door on his past and hang up his guns, but people wouldn't let him.

DONOVAN
Elmer Kelton

Donovan was supposed to be dead. Uncle Joe Vickers had fired off both barrels of a shotgun into the vicious outlaw's face as he was escaping from jail. Now Uncle Joe had been shot — in just the same way.

CODE OF THE GUN
Gordon D. Shirreffs

MacLean came riding home, with saddle tramp written all over him, but sewn in his shirt-lining was an Arizona Ranger's star.

GAMBLER'S GUN LUCK
Brett Austen

Gamblers seldom live long. Parker was a hell of a gambler. It was his life — or his death . . .

ORPHAN'S PREFERRED
Jim Miller

Sean Callahan answers the call of the Pony Express and fights Indians and outlaws to get the mail through.

DAY OF THE BUZZARD
T. V. Olsen

All Val Penmark cared about was getting the men who killed his wife.

THE MANHUNTER
Gordon D. Shirreffs

Lee Kershaw knew that every Rurale in the territory was on the lookout for him. But the offer of $5,000 in gold to find five small pieces of leather was too good to turn down.

RIFLES ON THE RANGE
Lee Floren

Doc Mike and the farmer stood there alone between Smith and Watson. There was this moment of stillness, and then the roar would start. And somebody would die . . .

HARTIGAN
Marshall Grover

Hartigan had come to Cornerstone to die. He chose the time and the place, and Main Street became a battlefield.

SUNDANCE: OVERKILL
John Benteen

When a wealthy banker's daughter was kidnapped by the Cheyenne, he offered Sundance $10,000 to rescue the girl.